Emma's Home

Book One
Of the Fairfield Series

By

Maryann Jordan

Emma's Home
Copyright © 2014 Maryann Jordan
Print Edition

All rights reserved. No part of this book may be reproduced or transmitted in any form or by any means, electronic or mechanical, including photocopying, recording, or by any information storage and retrieval system without the written permission of the author, except where permitted by law.

This book is a work of fiction. Names, characters, places, and incidents either are products of the author's imagination or are used fictitiously. Any resemblance to actual persons, living or dead, events, or locales is entirely coincidental.

Cover Design by: Kari Ayasha, Cover to Cover Designs
covertocoverdesigns.com

ISBN-13: 978-0-9916522-1-1
ISBN-10: 0991652215

Dedication

I dedicate this book to my family. My husband, Michael, who always believed in my dreams. My daughters, MaryBeth and Nicole, who are my inspiration. My daughter, Michelle, who I carry with me in my heart. Without you, I am nothing.

Prologue

Life can change in the blink of an eye. What we know, what we love – it can all change.

Our comfort, our security, our home – it can all be taken away.

One phone call can change everything. One phone call can take a well-ordered plan and leave us without a compass.

That's all it takes – one phone call. And then we are left to begin again, start over, find a new home.

In the blink of an eye.

Emma loved fall. It always felt as though life had taken on new colors as the summer green faded. The orange, yellow, and red leaves created a backdrop that brought the whole world alive. She walked across campus, basking in the fall sunlight, enjoying the walk to her early morning classes. The cool crispness made the air seem fresh after the heat of the summer. She lifted her face to the colors above, satisfied with her life.

Turning eighteen a few months ago, she had just started college. Her mother, a widowed mom, worked hard as a school secretary to make sure Emma could fulfill her dream of going to college.

Money had always been tight, and Emma was raised to understand the value of a dollar. When she was six years old, her sister Sarah, who was only sixteen at the time, gave birth to a beautiful baby girl named Laurie out of wedlock, and they continued to live at home with Emma's parents. Their parents supported Sarah during this time and actually loved having both of their daughters and their grand-daughter living with them. Emma's father passed away when she was only fourteen years old, and her mother had to continue her job to make the small amount of insurance money they received last to pay all of the bills.

Her savings, plus the scholarships that Emma worked hard to earn, had paid off, and now she was halfway through her first semester. She smiled as she looked at her surroundings. Unlike many of her fellow students, she never took the experience for granted, knowing all too well how much work and sacrifice had gone into the dream of her becoming a teacher. Walking toward the tall, stone building that housed the School of Education, Emma's cell phone in her backpack began to vibrate. Digging it out, she looked down and saw her mother's work number come up on the screen.

"Hey mom," she greeted.

"Emma? This is Mrs. Smithfield, your mom's principal." *How odd that she would be calling on mom's cell phone.*

"Is everything all right with my mom?" Emma asked. There was a pause. Fear trickled down Emma's spine. Her steps slowed to a crawl outside the classroom building as other students rushed by on their way inside.

"Emma, I am so sorry to have to tell you this, but your mom was in a car accident this morning. Sweetie, you need to come home."

"Is she okay?" Emma choked out.

"I really don't have any details, but you need to come home."

Emma hung up, then called her sister's cell phone with shaking hands. *Come on, Sarah. Pick up.* The call went straight to voicemail. Turning, Emma ran back to her dorm. Running into her room, she began throwing clothes into her suitcase. Her roommate looked up as Emma was rushing around the small room.

"My mom's been hurt. I've got to go home," Emma managed to get out.

"Do you need anything?" her roommate asked with true concern on her face.

"No, but thanks. Hopefully I'll be back soon."

Throwing her suitcase, laptop, book bag, and a few other items into her old car, she took off down the road. She ignored the colors of fall which just a few hours ago had brought her such enjoyment. Leaving the radio off, Emma was alone with her thoughts – thoughts that circled her mind like a tornado, leaving destruction in their path.

God, keep mom safe. Please keep her safe. She's all I've got. I can't lose her now.

During the two hour drive, she kept trying to call her sister, but all of the calls went to voicemail. Refusing to believe that anything bad had really happened, Emma flew down the road. By the time she was about fifteen minutes away, her phone finally rang again. Looking down to see Sarah's number, she punched the phone to answer.

"Sarah, thank God it is you. Is mom all right?" she asked, hands shaking on the steering wheel.

"Emma?" a small voice asked.

"Laurie?" Emma asked incredulously. "Is that you? Why are you on your mom's phone?"

"Emma," the voice cried. "Momma and grandma were hurt in the car today. The man says they aren't coming back."

"Laurie, where are you?" Emma shrieked into the phone. She heard shuffling in the background.

"Miss Dodd?" a man asked.

"Yes, this is Emma Dodd. Who is this? Where is my niece, Laurie?"

"Miss Dodd, this is Dr. Rocinni at Mercy General Hospital. I have your niece with me. She is fine. You need to come to the hospital as soon as you can."

"I'm just about ten minutes away. What is going on? Why did she say our mommas weren't coming back?" Emma asked as panic set in.

"I'm sorry Miss Dodd, I can tell you more when you get here."

Emma knew what he wasn't saying. She parked and ran in, seeing her twelve year old niece sitting with some nurses. Emma felt the horror before the doctor confirmed her worst nightmare. Her mom and sister were not coming back from the car crash. Emma was aware that life as she knew it was over. But before she could allow the emotions to take her under, she scooped up her niece, holding her close.

The next day as she was struggling to make funeral arrangements, she also had to meet with a county social worker. It never entered Emma's mind that she would not be with Laurie, but she was going to have to prove to be the most acceptable guardian, or Laurie could be made a ward of the state. The social worker was sympathetic, but explained that she had to have Laurie's best interests at heart.

"Where is Laurie's father?" she asked, her forms neatly held in her clipboard.

Emma stared at the clipboard. All of the papers were stacked so neatly. *This woman wants our life to fit on her forms. Neat. Orderly. All the boxes checked. But what if they don't?* Nauseous, Emma clasped her hand over her mouth, certain that she would be sick. Fighting the bile threatening to come up, Emma kept staring at the clipboard.

"Are you all right?" the social worker asked. Emma just nodded in response. "I do need to know about Laurie's father. What can you tell me about him and how to contact him?" she continued.

"We don't know his name."

At this the social worker looked up from her forms, a questioning expression on her face.

Taking a deep breath, Emma plunged forward. "My sister was only sixteen. She was a really good girl," she said, the pleading for understanding straining her voice. "But she met a soldier on leave. She didn't know his name. She had no way of telling him. There is no father listed on the birth certificate."

With tears falling down Emma's face she suddenly realized that she could lose everyone. "You can't take her from me," she cried. "We've been like sisters since the day she was born. I have changed her, rocked her, held her, played with her….. I am all that she has now. You take her away from me and you take away the only family she has left…. you take away the only family I have left."

The social worker with the kind eyes looked at Emma and said, "Well, you are a legal adult, but I have to be able to prove that you can support her. As soon as you get the funeral over with, we will need to meet and go over your plan. I have to see your finances, where you will live, and what resources you will have."

All of her words seemed jumbled to Emma's grief-stricken mind.

But at least she didn't say 'no'. That must mean something.

Simply nodding, Emma assured her that she would do whatever was necessary to become Laurie's guardian.

Two days later, standing at the gravesite of her mother and sister, Emma held Laurie's little hand. The warm fall sun shown down on the ones left behind. The white grave stones all around stood out in stark relief to the fall colors. Emma stood in front of the coffins, surrounded by friends and neighbors there to pay respects to two beautiful ladies. Emma found herself staring at the knobs of the coffins. The flowers on top. The way the funeral staff covered the gaping holes in the ground with a green carpet to resemble real grass. The finality of the situation began to seep in, chilling her in spite of the warm sun.

Her mind swirled as much as the multicolored leaves above.

Oh mom, why did you have to go? I'm not ready to lose you now. I have no idea what I am doing. I don't know how to live without you guiding me.

Oh Sarah, I have lost my best friend as well as sister. What will I do without you? How will I ever be able to be as good of a mom to Laurie as you were?

Oh God, hear my prayer. Help me.

Laurie looked up at Emma with tears running down her face, hiccupping occasionally. Emma pulled her in closer. Laurie and Emma were now both orphans. All alone. Except for each other.

Chapter 1

13 years later

Emma watched the scenery fly by as she drove down the road toward her destination. The hot summer sun beat down, and her hair blew away from her face with the air conditioner on full blast. Having lived in the south her whole life, she still found the heat of the Virginia summers to be oppressive. The green foliage shimmered in the heat waves coming from the road. There was more traffic than she would have liked with all of the vacation travelers. She watched them in their huge SUVs loaded down with luggage, bicycles, some even pulling campers. Emma thought back to the one vacation she had ever taken as an adult. She and Laurie had gone to the beach when Laurie graduated from high school. Emma had saved up just enough money for them to take a road trip and spend two nights in a hotel. Lying on the beach and swimming in the waves had been glorious. Laurie had been grateful, but Emma wished that she could have given her more.

With the radio blaring in her old car, she smiled to herself as she thought of where she was headed. Life had not always been easy, but she made the best of it. At the age of eighteen, Emma was granted guardianship of her niece, Laurie. The insurance money only covered funeral expenses, so they sold the house. Moving to an apartment over the restaurant where she worked allowed Laurie to be looked after when Emma was working the evening shift. Emma took college classes during the day when Laurie was in school and spent her afternoons with Laurie. The restaurant owner's mother would watch over Laurie in the evenings when Emma was working. Now at only thirty one, her life had certainly not been what she dreamed it would be, but looking back she couldn't help but smile as she thought of all she had accomplished. She and Laurie made it through college, although it took longer than most students. Both loving education, Laurie had graduated in Elementary Education and had landed a job last year in the small town of Fairfield, about three hours away from Emma. They tried for one year to live apart, but some relationships in life just need to stay physically close to feel as though life is balanced. Laurie had begged Emma to come live in Fairfield as well. Emma liked her job as a high school counselor, but found that she missed Laurie more and more. So she turned in her notice once she secured a new job in Fairfield at their high school. Emma put her furniture in storage and told an ecstatic Laurie that she was moving.

Pulling her car off the highway at a rest stop, she needed a quick break. With only a little farther to go to her destination, she wanted to be as fresh as possible when seeing her niece again. She hoped Laurie would keep the greeting simple, but her niece was the type to throw a party. Well, best be prepared. Using the ladies room, she touched up her makeup and ran her fingers through her hair. Giving up on that, she realized there was no one to make an impression on. Sliding back into her car, she continued down the road.

She was finally off the highway and on smaller, less congested roads. Emma enjoyed the view of the mountains as they rose up in the foreground. She had never lived near the mountains and loved the vista in front of her.

Fairfield..... it sounds like a nice place for a home.

"You're meeting us tonight at Smokey's, right?" Laurie said on phone.

"Yeah, yeah, I'll be there," Jake answered.

"My aunt is coming in this evening, and I want her to meet all of us at the bar so she can know some people in town." Silence greeted her. "You'll like her, I promise." More silence. "Jake, just be her date for the evening since the rest of us are paired off." More silence. "Are you there?" she asked.

"I'll be there. Later," was the only answer she received. Laurie glanced over at her boyfriend, Rob, who was grinning. Rob was lying back on the couch, watching baseball. He was tall, muscular from years of football and now as a firefighter. He kept his dark hair short, saying that it was too hot for long hair under a fire helmet. Laurie walked over and snuggled up against him on the couch.

"You tryin' to set Jake up with your aunt?" Rob asked. Laurie answered with a laugh. Rob continued, "Babe, he's gonna walk in thinkin' he's been set up with some little old lady as his date. You think that's fair?"

"He should know she's not old. I'm sure I've talked about her before," Laurie answered.

"Laurie, you talking and a guy listening are two different things. Most of the time, we just tune you girls out and nod occasionally."

Laurie looked up with an incredulous look on her face. "Well, if he hasn't been listening, that's not my fault!" She leaned up and pulled her hair into a messy bun.

Rob looked at her profile as she was fingering her hair. Laurie was petite but curvy, and when she leaned back in to snuggle, she fit perfectly next to him.

Laurie leaned back over to Rob, pressing into his chest to give him a quick kiss. "It'll be fun, you'll see."

Rob dipped down and deepened the kiss. Turning her quick peck into a soul searing, kiss, he kept her from plotting any more matchmaking plans with their friends.

෴

Jake slipped his cell phone back into his pocket. "Damn," he said under his breath.

"What's eatin' at you?" said his partner. Jake and Tom had been paired up as detectives for the Fairfield Police for the past several years, and had been friends since childhood. He, Tom, and Rob had been friends, football teammates, and now lived in the same town as adults.

"Laurie," Jake answered while Tom laughed.

"She still settin' you up with her aunt at Smokey's tonight? Come on, Jake. It will be fun."

"Fuck off," Jake said. "You don't have to show up at the town's main bar with a date the age of your mom." Tom would be there with his wife, Carol.

"Look, it is just for dinner tonight, so she can meet some people. That's all."

"Yeah, I know," Jake answered. He stood up from his desk, stretching his six foot two inch muscular frame, rolling his neck to ease the tension. "It's not really Laurie or her aunt comin' into town. I'd just rather go home and chill tonight. Not much in the mood to be around everyone."

Tom nodded, looking back at the files on his desk. They had been working on a robbery case and were getting nowhere. The missing items were not all that important, but considering that the robbery had taken place at the high school, the department was on alert. The case was several days old, and they had very few leads. The principal was friends with the mayor and results were expected quickly. There were no signs of breaking and entering, so the police were running into dead ends.

"Come on – let's head out," Tom said. "It's Friday night, and we need to go hit the bars with our ladies," he smirked. "I'm runnin' home to change and get Carol. We'll see you at Smokey's."

Jake dropped by his mom's house to shower and change. He took off his badge and gun holster and laid them on his dresser. Coming out of the shower, he chose faded jeans and a black t-shirt that stretched across his chest. He kept in shape working out 3 times a week at the local gym and running every morning before going to the station. He had never had a problem attracting women but was cautious about sleeping around. Fairfield wasn't a small town, but neither was it a large metropolis. He had no desire to run into previous one night stands while on the job. Before Tom met Carol, Tom had no such cares and had his fair share of one night conquests. Afterwards, Tom instantly gave up his man whore ways and was completely whipped.

Their friend Rob, a local firefighter/EMT had met his girlfriend, Laurie, when there was a fire at the elementary school where she was a new teacher. All three were over six feet tall and turned the ladies' eyes whenever they made an appearance. But since Laurie and Carol had entered the scene, Jake was often the odd man out, unless he brought a date.

It wasn't as though Jake did not want a relation-ship – he just had not found the right woman yet. Finding a woman who would meet his standards and understand his life choices was difficult. Usually as soon as a woman found out that he was thirty-three years old and living in his mother's house, she would declare that a deal breaker and not come around again. He had his reasons, and if a woman couldn't understand his situation, then he wasn't interested in her either. But it made life a little lonely.

Looking in the mirror before heading out, the thought that he certainly wouldn't be finding the love of his life tonight went through his head. He knew he was running late, but what the hell, he had no one to impress. Sighing to himself, Jake left his room.

Mary Campbell looked up smiling as Jake came down the stairs. She was sitting in a comfortable chair, her Kindle in her lap. "Hey sweetheart, are you heading out now?" she asked. She wished that his father could have seen what a wonderful man Jake was. Her son looked so much like her late husband that she sometimes had to pinch herself to remember who she was looking at. Jake's father would have been so proud of him, just as she was.

"Yeah, mom. Are you going to be all right here tonight? I may be late, but I can easily cut this evening short. In fact, I may want to cut it short," he added, ruefully rubbing his hands through his thick sandy colored hair.

"Of course," Mary replied. "I don't have to go upstairs for anything, and I have my walker right next to my chair if I need it. Have a good time."

Leaning down, Jake kissed his mother on the cheek before he headed out of the door. Jake's dad had been diagnosed with cancer soon after Jake had graduated from the police academy, and he came back to Fairfield to help out. Soon after his dad passed away, his mother was diagnosed with rheumatoid arthritis, and was having difficulty taking care of things by herself. Jake moved out of his apartment and back into her home to help out. He did not begrudge his choices, but knew that it would take a very special woman to ever be able to have a relationship with him. He sighed deeply and headed downtown to the bar.

ॐ

Laurie, Rob, Tom, and Carol were sitting at a table in the back of the bar where there was more room to move around. Emma had arrived about thirty minutes earlier, much to the delight of Laurie.

Smokey's had a homey feel with rich dark wood on the floor and the bar. Behind the bar was an old fashioned mirror with brass light fixtures. Tables and booths lined one side and were in the back, along with an area for a few pool tables. Smokey's also served great food, one of the reasons Laurie chose this as their meeting place. The bar was run by

Wendy and Bill Evans, longtime town residents, who knew everyone and everything going on in the town.

"God, I can't believe you are finally here and not just visiting but staying!" Laurie said while not letting go of Emma's hands. Laurie, like Emma, was petite but her thick brown hair hung in soft waves down her back. Emma was a brunette with auburn highlights that fell to just below her shoulders. Emma had the dark brown eyes of her parents, but Laurie's were stormy grey, a trait they could only assume came from her father.

"It was time for a change, and I figured I might as well come to where my only family was," Emma replied, smiling at her niece.

Seeing Laurie sitting next to Rob, Emma noticed the way they looked at each other. Rob was tall and powerfully built. He wore faded jeans, a navy t-shirt fitted tightly to his torso, and cowboy boots.

"Rob, I'm so glad to meet you. I can tell by the way Laurie is looking at you, this is the real deal," Emma said enthusiastically.

"I'm the lucky one," Rob replied, smiling back at the lady who had given up everything to raise the woman he loved.

Carol and Tom sat across from Emma. Carol was a beautiful slim woman with blonde hair stylishly cut to just below her shoulders. She had an angelic aura about her. Her husband, Tom, was slightly leaner than Rob, with the same yellow blond hair that his wife had. Carol wiggled in her seat, trying to disguise the rumbling of her stomach. Her husband gazed at her with a questioning look on his face.

"I'm sorry, I'm just really hungry. I haven't eaten since breakfast," Carol said sheepishly.

Laurie looked around, not seeing Jake. "I wanted to wait and order when Jake got here. Where *is* he?" she said, agitated. Tom and Rob shared a look over their wives' heads.

Emma grinned. "Am I being stood up, gentle-men?" Emma, never taking herself too seriously, knew that life was too precious to waste on things that just did not matter. And being stood up by a man she had never met would certainly not break her.

Laurie snapped her head around, looking up at Rob to see what she was missing. Her temper began to rise, but Rob quickly spoke to calm her.

"He would never skip out – he knows how important this dinner is to you."

"Yeah," Tom added. "He's just running late."

"Well, while we are waiting on him, why don't you go ahead and order appetizers? I am going to run to the ladies room." Emma stood and walked over toward the hall by the bar.

Chapter 2

J ake pulled his pickup truck up to the bar, but didn't get out right away. He didn't know why he was so opposed to going inside to have dinner with his friends. He understood he wasn't being "set up" with Laurie's aunt; he was just supposed to meet her and sit with her so she would have a dinner partner. But being there watching Rob and Tom have what he wanted was just going to be one more reason for delaying. He was happy his friends had found amazing, beautiful women. Rob and Tom were his best friends and deserved the best. But… Jake shook his head to clear his thoughts. Taking a deep breath, he hopped out of his truck.

Approaching the door to the bar, he saw a tall, skinny blonde with painted on blue jeans, hanging around the front. Recognizing the young woman as Brandi, a notorious flirt always looking for attention, he tried to walk by. She turned around, a huge hungry smile covering her face.

"Jake," she purred. "I was supposed to meet someone, but he isn't here yet, so you can buy me a drink." She latched onto his arm, dragging a long red fingernail down his chest.

"Sorry, Brandi, but I am meeting friends," he said as he tried to disentangle himself.

"Well, since you didn't come with anyone, I can be your date," she said as they walked inside the bar.

Brandi, barely old enough to drink legally, was too young to be a barfly, but Jake knew that her father always asked the bar owner Bill, to keep an eye on her.

Not wanting to be seen with Brandi and knowing Laurie would be furious if she saw her, Jake took her firmly by the arms and pushed her back. "Brandi, I'm not your date. I'm here to meet Laurie's aunt. You need to go find your friends."

"Her aunt?" Brandi laughed. "You don't want some old lady for your date!"

∾

Turning, Jake glimpsed his friends sitting at the back. He started towards them, but a movement near the bar caught his eye. A petite brunette with tight jeans that cupped a luscious ass was walking by the bar.

That's new. I'd sure have remembered her if I'd seen her before!

Damn, of all the times to be unavailable, this would be the night that he saw someone that made his pulse quicken. His eyes followed the woman as she turned and headed toward the back of the bar. He glimpsed enough of her profile to see that her tits were as luscious as her ass. The mystery woman stopped at Laurie's table.

Not seeing an older woman sitting at the table, he decided to get over there quickly to meet the new woman, before having to meet Laurie's aunt. As he approached the table, the mystery woman turned around.

Jake found himself looking down into sparkling eyes as dark as chocolate and a full mouth just made for kissing. Her dark brown hair hung in waves below her shoulders, auburn highlights shining under the barroom lights, and he instantly thought of what it would feel like to tangle his hands in her hair as he took her. She was petite, probably only a couple of inches over five feet, but up close he could see the curves that he had noticed over by the bar. Her light pink top was clingy but not slutty and scooped down in the front just enough that he could glimpse the tops of her breasts.

The beauty standing in front of him looked up and smiled a genuine smile that lit her whole face. Jake couldn't remember the last time he had seen such a look of unadulterated joy aimed at him. He could actually *feel* her smile deep inside.

Emma couldn't believe how far up she had to look to see his face. He must be a foot taller than her and she scanned the masculine beauty towering over her. His eyes were the most beautiful blue eyes she had ever seen and his broad shoulders tapered down to trim hips. His black t-shirt was pulled tightly over his muscular chest and his bulging arms by his sides made her wonder what they would be like wrapped around her. Her eyes traveled down, noticing the fit of his jeans at his crotch and the muscular thighs stretching the jean material. Emma's eyes continued their downward appraisal, ending with the cowboy boots on his feet.

Laurie's voice carried over the jukebox music. "Jake, I'd like you to meet my aunt Emma and Emma, this is Jake."

This is her date for the evening? Emma couldn't believe her luck.

What? Laurie's aunt? Jake was so stunned that he couldn't even move. He just stood there dumbly staring. The smile seemed to drop from her face as her eyes searched his.

Before anyone could say anything, a voice beside him screeched, "You don't look like some old lady." Emma's eyes quickly cut over to the very young blond Barbie doll holding on to Jake's arm.

Laurie was furious. "What the hell are you doing here, Brandi?"

Brandi, oblivious to the glares coming her way, just stared at Emma in surprise. "Jake didn't want to come in and be some ol' lady's date, but you don't look old at all!"

Everyone sat for a moment in stunned silence. Emma, with a raised eyebrow, just looked from Jake to Brandi and then threw her head back and laughed. Not a sultry, fake laugh that some women use when they are trying to seduce a man, but a real laugh.

"Well thank you, I think," Emma said. "I do believe I'll take that as a compliment!"

Then chaos erupted. Laurie was so incensed at the insult to Emma she stood up ready to kick Brandi's ass. Carol was equally ready to jump into the fray. Rob stood, put his hands on Laurie's shoulders and pulled her back down. Tom shushed Carol and pulled her into his lap. Both Tom and

Rob looked over at Jake, trying to understand how in the hell he could have walked in with Brandi when he was supposed to meet Emma. All the while, Jake and Emma just looked at each other while Brandi had gone on to her next thought.

"Oh my God. Are those Smokey's' hot wings?" Brandi squealed. "I love those!" She pushed her way passed Emma, knocking her into Jake, plopping down in Emma's chair.

Jake grabbed Emma's shoulders to keep her from stumbling. The touch sparked between them and she turned her eyes back up to Jake in surprise.

Jake was equally surprised. The only emotion he felt when Brandi's arm was wrapped around his, was discomfort. But one accidental touch from Emma had him feeling alive. He could feel the blood heading south to his dick, but he forced himself to get those thoughts of Emma out of his head.

She's a lady, and a tiny one at that. The last thing she needs is to see my hard on, straining in my jeans when we just met.

Jake had had enough of Brandi's interference. He reluctantly released his hold on Emma's shoulders, moving forward to haul Brandi out of Emma's chair, but Emma jumped in to stop him.

"Oh please, let her sit. Here you sit with your... uh...date," Emma said with a smirk, pointing to the chair next to Brandi. "I'll find another chair."

Before he knew what was happening, Emma had hurried over and pulled another chair by Laurie and Rob. Jake was furious. For a man who always liked to be in charge, he felt totally pushed around at the moment, first by Laurie, then by Brandi, and now by this pint-sized beauty who seemed to be finding the whole situation amusing.

"Well, now that introductions have been taken care of, let's eat," Tom said, trying to diffuse the situation and calm his wife who was still steaming. Rob, taking the hint, quickly agreed and waved the waitress over. Brandi, oblivious as ever, continued to fill her plate with hot wings, as the stares back and forth between the six other people at the table bounced all around. Laurie pulled out her cell phone, scrolling through her contacts.

"Who are you trying to call?" Rob asked, leaning over her shoulder to see the screen.

Laurie looked directly at Jake when she answered. "Mike. I thought I would see if he was free tonight to join us."

Mike was another one of their unattached friends who worked with Jake and Tom on the police force. Mike was a good looking guy, and Jake knew exactly what Laurie was trying to do; he would be damned before he let her set Emma up with someone else. He may have made an error in judgment when it came to meeting Emma, but planned on rectifying that as soon as he could.

"Mike's on duty tonight," Jake spoke up.

Laurie looked frustrated as she slid her phone back into her pocket.

Tom looked over at Jake; he knew Mike wasn't on duty. Tom chuckled, knowing exactly what Jake had done. Mike was known as a player, and Jake was making sure that Emma wasn't going to be his next conquest.

Emma smiled at the table full of friends, deciding that she was going to like Fairfield.

"So I know Laurie works at the elementary school, and Rob works as a firefighter. What about you all?" she said in her slightly southern drawl.

Carol, who was still shooting daggers at Brandi, looked over at Emma and smiled. "I'm a nurse over at Fairfield Hospital, and Tom is a detective with the Fairfield Police," she said as she adoringly looked up at her husband.

Looking at the two couples sitting at the table, Emma could not help but have a pang of envy. With their beautiful women, Tom and Rob looked happy. She spared a glance at Jake and Barbie doll – *okay, that's not fair* she admonished herself, *the girl's name is Brandi.*

"And you two?" she asked.

Jake, jaw tight, growled, "We're not together."

"Okaaay," Emma said, trying to hold in a smile. "But I still would like to know more about you."

Before Jake could growl again, Tom quickly spoke up. "Jake is my partner."

"That's wonderful," Emma exclaimed, "I feel safe! Two detectives and a firefighter!" They laughed and the tension around the table seemed to loosen.

Jake couldn't help but look over at Emma; the smile on her face reached her eyes as she looked around their group of friends. She was definitely different from many women he knew. Most women would have been incensed that their date was sitting with another woman, but she seemed to take it all in stride. He glanced at Brandi, who still oblivious to the mess she had caused, was now sitting back twirling her hair and looking around. Laurie, who had finally calmed down, was holding Emma's hand and smiling.

Carol turned to them. "I just have to ask you two – how is it that you are so young and yet you raised Laurie? You look like sisters, not aunt and niece!"

Laurie and Emma smiled at each other, years of understanding passing between them.

Laurie smiled, nodding to Emma. "You can tell our story. We're all friends here."

"Well, Laurie's mother was my sister, although she was about ten years older than I was." Laughing,

Emma confessed, "My parents used to call me their 'oops' baby. I was only six years old when Laurie was born, and they lived with us. My father died when I was a teenager so for a while it was just a house full of girls. So, you see, Laurie and I were raised very much like sisters." Emma smiled. "In fact, I thought Laurie was my live doll baby."

Laurie, taking over the story, continued, "That's right! I grew up always being dressed up in cute clothes!"

"So that's where the 'I need more clothes' comes from," Rob joked. They all laughed, knowing how Laurie loved clothes.

"Hey, you can't blame that on me!" exclaimed Emma.

"Please continue," Carol pleaded.

"Well, when I was eighteen, I went to college about an hour away from home. I was about halfway through the first semester when I was called home." Emma's smile left her face, and she reached over to take Laurie's hand again. Jake, as a detective had been trained to read people's faces. He knew whatever was coming next was important. He was interested to see what Emma would say.

"My mom and Sarah were killed in a car accident." No one spoke. Laurie wiped a tear from her cheek as Rob pulled her in for a hug.

"So it was just Laurie and I left," Emma stated.

"But you were only eighteen… how did you take care of her?" Carol interjected.

Emma looked up, smiling. "Well," she drawled, "I was the only living relative, so of course I became her guardian."

She stated this so matter of factly, Jake wondered if Emma even realized how amazing it was.

"I left college and moved back home. The insurance money helped us keep the house for a little while and then we decided to sell it because we needed the money."

"You gave up college?" Tom asked. He was only saying out loud what the others were thinking. How could an eighteen year old change her life so quickly and take on raising a twelve year old?

Emma looked up in surprise. "She needed me." And then she smiled and looked over at Laurie. "And I needed her."

The table was quiet for a moment. Jake stared at the beautiful woman sitting at the end of the table, wishing more than ever that she was sitting next to him. He wanted to wrap his arms around her, holding her close. He felt a desire to protect her and take care of her the way she cared for others, recognizing how special she was.

Right then, Brandi popped her gum loudly, breaking the silence. While the others glared at her, Emma just threw her head back and laughed. Jake thought it was the most refreshing sound he had ever heard.

"I did not give up college completely," Emma explained. "It just took longer. I transferred to the community college and took a few classes at a time. When I could, I finished at the university closest to us. I had a job to help support us, so we did fine."

Jake continued to stare. The life change that most people would not have chosen to make, seemed to totally unfazed Emma. They had celebrated Laurie's twenty fifth birthday a few months past, so that would make Emma only thirty-one… hardly the older woman he was prepared to meet considering he was thirty three years old himself.

"Oh my God!" exclaimed Brandi. "I couldn't have given up my life for a kid!"

Jake growled as the others glared. He glanced over at Emma to see if she was upset.

Emma leaned forward, looking directly at Brandi with a sincere smile on her face. "Well, my dear, I think we can all be glad that you never had to make that choice," she said trying not to laugh.

Brandi, oblivious as ever, sat back and huffed. "I'm bored, Jakey. Let's go shoot some pool."

Jake turned in his seat, his patience over, and leaned into her face. "For the last time Brandi, I. Am. Not. Here. With. You."

Laurie had had all she was going to take. "Brandi, no one invited you. This is a private gathering so get the hell away from our table!"

Brandi, unused to men not fawning over her, waited for them to jump to her defense. When it did not happen, she pushed her chair back and stomped over to the pool tables.

"Fine, I did not want to sit with a bunch of boring old foggies anyway." she shouted over her shoulder.

"Laurie!" Emma admonished, "You shouldn't have pushed her away on my account."

All of the eyes at the table turned towards her, beginning to talk at once, assuring her they were better off without Brandi's company.

"Well, I *was* getting a little tired of being called old," Emma laughed. She looked over and caught Jake staring at her. His eyes never wavered from hers; she usually could hold her own in a stare down, but found herself feeling self-conscious. Maybe he thinks I *am* old.

The food finally arrived and conversation flowed again.

"So you're staying with Laurie?" Carol assumed.

"No way!" Emma exclaimed.

"What?" Laurie yelled. "Of course you are staying with us!"

"Laurie, you and Rob just moved in together. You think I would intrude?" Emma asked. Rob and Laurie assured her that they wanted her there, but Emma stood firm. She insisted that she was staying in the little hotel down the street near the bar. "In fact, I have already checked in, put my bags in the room, met the delightful owners, and checked out the hotel pool for a swim later on!" she laughed.

Jake snapped his head around quickly and looked over at her. *What the hell?* The thought of Emma in a swimsuit in the hotel's outdoor pool in the middle of the night made his blood run cold. Fairfield may be a small town, but it had its share of crime. He hated the thought of her being in a swimsuit without him around for protection.

Fuck, who am I kidding? I just don't want anyone else to see her luscious body besides me.

"You're not swimming later tonight," he stated as though that would be the end of the conversation. He didn't ask, he just stated.

"Sure I am, the pool is heated."

"You're not swimming at night," he stated again, not taking his eyes off of her.

"Uh oh, the protector is coming out in him," Laurie interjected.

"I don't care what is coming out of him, no one tells me what to do," Emma declared. It was hard to stare at all of that male beauty glaring at her, but she forced her libido to take a back seat to her irritation.

"Jake's used to getting his way," Carol explained as though that should make it all right.

"Well, so am I! And at my *advanced* years, I hardly think I need anyone to tell me what to do!" said Emma.

"Fuck!" Jake growled, scooting his chair back quickly and walking over toward the bar. He knew he had screwed up the minute he thought that Laurie's aunt was an older woman and he allowed Brandi to walk in with him. That gorgeous, infuriating brunette sitting back at the table was not going to make things easy, and all he wanted right now was to jerk her out of the chair, push her up against the wall, and kiss her until she couldn't think anymore. He headed through the crowded room toward the bar to get another beer and cool down. Never one to lose control, he couldn't believe how quickly Emma had gotten under his skin. Well, she may have thought she won this round, but he never backed down from a challenge.

Rob and Tom looked over and grinned at each other. Jake had always held himself apart from having a relationship, saying that he couldn't take care of his mom and have a girlfriend at the same time, although Tom and Rob tried to convince him differently. Rob always said one day someone would come along who would knock Jake on his ass.

Emma couldn't decide if she was more irritated at Jake for trying to be bossy or for walking away. All she knew was that after the long drive, she was too tired to think about the gorgeous man who had walked over to the bar. As she said her goodbyes to the rest of their group, Rob and Laurie invited them all over for a barbeque soon. Walking through the crowd toward the door of the bar, she felt eyes boring into the back of her. Turning around she saw Jake staring at her. She held his stare for a moment before giving a sad little smile and a halfhearted wave in his direction. Jake nodded her way, his eyes never leaving hers.

Damn, he's gorgeous, she thought. *Too bad he's not interested.*

Damn, she's gorgeous, he thought. *And I'm just the man for her.*

Chapter 3

Emma, too keyed up to go right to sleep, decided to take a quick swim. She changed into her old faded, one piece black swimsuit, took out her contacts, grabbed her glasses and a towel, and headed out. She swam laps for about thirty minutes then decided she was tired enough to go back to her room. Climbing out of the pool, she looked around for her towel. Realizing she was on the opposite side from where she left it, she started to walk around the pool's edge.

"You just couldn't resist, could you?" resonated a deep voice several feel away. Emma jumped back with a squeak, panic written on her face.

"Who's there?" she squinted in the dim light, trying to see. Jake looked down at the table holding her towel and saw her glasses.

Furious, he growled, "You come out here in the middle of the night, and you can't even see around you without your glasses?"

Emma was too startled to speak. He reached down, snagged her towel and glasses, and stalked toward her.

"Jake, what are you doing out here?"

He stared at the water droplets falling from her hair, running down her shoulders, and down her breasts. *What would I give to be one of those drops of water right now?*

Realizing that he was staring, he wrapped the towel around her shoulders, shielding her beautiful distracting body from his view. He placed her glasses on her face, and looked into her eyes. Jake could see by her expression that she was gearing up for an argument. Not wanting to hear it, he bent, scooped her up in his powerful arms, and carried her over his shoulders up to her room.

"Jake, put me down," Emma whispered, not wanting to wake any of the hotel's residents. Jake's only response was a slap on her swimsuit covered ass. Once at her door, he pulled out her room card from his pocket, which he had palmed while she was swimming. Throwing open the door, he lowered her to the floor gently.

"What were you thinking?" He bent down to look her eye to eye. "You're new in town, hardly know anyone, don't have your cell phone with you, swimming in a hotel pool in the middle of the night, blind as a bat, where anyone could grab you, and you'd never see them coming."

Emma's heart was racing, but she wasn't sure if it was from being angry or being in such close proximity to Jake. She couldn't remember ever being this near to such a virile, handsome man…and one who was equally infuriating. The cold room was making her nipples poke through her swimsuit. She tried to clutch the wet towel around her tighter.

Jake was aware of how little Emma had on. Although having seen much more skin from women wearing tiny bikinis, he was entranced by how beautiful she looked in her one piece suit. Her wet hair was slicked back from her face; she had no makeup on and yet as he stared down into her dark eyes, he could not help but notice the pure beauty of her face. He could see that her nipples had pebbled, from the cold or from excitement he didn't know. He actually didn't care what the reason was; he just knew that he was growing hard at the thought of peeling her wet suit slowly from her body and discovering all of Emma's beauty. Shifting his stance, he attempted to hide the tightness in his jeans.

"And while we're at it, a man grabs you and starts to carry you off and you only whisper? You don't yell your head off?" Jake asked incredulously, crossing his huge arms over his impressive chest, staring down at her.

Taking a deep breath to calm herself, Emma looked up at Jake. "First of all, I didn't scream because I know you. I may have been upset at your high-handed way of carrying me, but I wasn't afraid of you. Should I have been?" she asked, looking up into his baby blue eyes. "And to answer your first question, well… I've always taken care of myself, Jake." She expected him to continue to argue or get angry.

Leaning over, he softly said, "Well, now you have someone to take care of you," as he kissed her forehead. "Lock up behind me." With that, he walked out the door.

Emma stunned by the evening's events, couldn't help but smile. Moving to Fairfield was definitely the right move.

The next week flew by as Emma discovered the town of Fairfield. Since her counseling job did not begin until the fall with the start of school, she and Laurie had time to visit shops and meet more of Laurie's friends. Emma became friendly with Helen and Roger, the couple who ran the hotel. They were in their mid-sixties, showing no signs of slowing down. Helen was a plump woman with her grey hair always pulled back into a bun. She reminded Emma of pictures of Mrs. Santa Claus. Roger was spry and wiry, always running around making sure the old hotel was fit for his guests, as he liked to say.

They regaled Emma with tales of the people who came through Fairfield and stayed at their hotel, often accompanied with pictures they had taken with their favorite guests. There were pictures lining the walls of the lobby of Helen and Roger through the years with an odd assortment of people. Each year a motorcycle group rode through and always had their picture taken with Helen and Roger. There were some families that came every year and stayed on their way to the state park nearby. Emma, walking around looking at the photographs, spotted an occasional politician and even a movie star whose limo had broken down in town one year. Roger told Emma that he wanted a picture of her on their wall.

Emma just laughed and told him that she wasn't famous enough to be in their esteemed collection.

Helen leaned over the counter and grasped Emma's hand. "Oh my dear, I have a feeling you are going to be so good for this town."

Emma, not knowing what to say, just mumbled, "Thank you."

Helen patted her hand and replied, "You'll see, my dear. You'll see."

Emma looked into Roger's smiling face. He winked at her and noted, "My Helen, she knows things, Emma. She can always tell the good ones from the bad ones. And she knows you are definitely one of the good ones."

In the mornings, Emma stopped by their office to share a cup of coffee. Roger walked to the coffee shop and bakery that was just down the street. He called it his morning constitutional for keeping in shape, which made Helen roll her eyes. After Roger left the office, Helen declared that she did not know why he walked to the bakery for exercise, only to fill up his belly with pastries. Emma giggled, enjoying the loving banter between these two.

At the bakery, the pastries were freshly baked each day, and the coffee was so much better than the franchise shops. Bernie's Bakery was owned by Bernadette, Rob's mom.

One day, sitting in the hotel office with Roger and Helen enjoying the coffee and pastries, Emma saw a picture of a teenager on their desk. She asked who the handsome young man was.

"That's our grandson, Brad," Roger answered proudly. "You'll see him once you start working – he goes to the high school where you will be."

"He is just as handsome as his grandfather," Emma noted. "How old is he?"

Roger, smiling at the compliment, had to think for a second. "Sweet pea, how old is Brad now? Is he fifteen or sixteen?" he yelled towards the back of the office where Helen was working on the books.

"He's almost eighteen," Emma heard Helen reply from the back.

Roger just shook his head. "I don't know where the years go! It seems just yesterday his mom, Wendy, was that age." Emma leaned over the counter and patted his hand.

She smiled and said, "I feel the same about Laurie."

"How do you feel about me?" Laurie asked as she walking into the office, looking amazing as always. Laurie was dressed in white capris with a pale yellow peasant blouse, just low enough to show off a hint of cleavage. Always conscious of being short, she paired her outfit with matching yellow wedge sandals with a four inch heel. Laurie had her hair pulled up in a high pony tail, knowing it was going to be a scorcher of a day.

Emma hugged her. "We were just noticing how quickly the years are passing."

"Oh God, surely you don't feel old yet?" Laurie asked. Laurie always felt a little guilty that Emma had given up so many years to raise her, even though she knew Emma dearly loved her.

"No, I don't feel old! Well, at least not as old as some people think I am!" she laughed.

"Emma, you are never going to let Jake live that down!" Laurie giggled. "Anyway, I am here to take to you Bernie's Bakery to pick up stuff to take to the firehouse. I told Rob we would visit this morning."

Emma and Laurie hopped into Laurie's yellow VW bug and headed down the street. The shops were starting to open, and Emma liked the friendly small town feel of downtown Fairfield. There were lots of strip malls on the outskirts of Fairfield, but Emma appreciated the quaintness of the downtown area. They parked and walked towards the bakery.

Emma and Laurie made quite a pair walking down the street, turning the eyes of several men passing them. Emma was dressed in robin's-egg blue shorts paired with a white eyelet tank top, both hugging her curves. Her dark brown hair swung around her shoulders, complimented the subtle makeup she wore. She had never gained the confidence that Laurie had wearing high heels, so Emma's three-inch white wedges did not give her much height, but her toned legs looked amazing nonetheless.

The happy pair entered the bakery. Emma met Bernie, Rob's mom and had the chance to chat with her for a little bit before they headed over to the firehouse. Bernie was a force to be reckoned with. She was a middle-age dynamo, bagging pastries and yelling out coffee orders to her barista for all the customers in line. Bernie had the same black hair that her son Rob had, with only a few sprinkles of gray. Her eyes were bright and friendly, and she looked like the type of person who never met a stranger. Her shop was welcoming, and Emma had a chance to look around before they picked up the food.

Images of a cup of hot coffee surrounded by cupcakes decorated the bright pink awning. The pink theme continued inside the shop. The chairs were all painted white and while the table legs were also white, the table tops were painted pastel pink. The soft pink walls were filled with pictures of pastries that immediately made customers want to indulge. The counter ran along one side of the shop; the glass cases filled to the brim with cookies, cupcakes, muffins, and other assorted goodies. The smell of homemade pastries baking in the back made Emma's mouth water.

"Are you sure we have to take goodies to the firehouse?" she joked to Laurie. "Can't we sit here and eat them all ourselves?"

Laughing, Laurie answered back. "I know! When I come in here, I know I am going to gain weight just by breathing!"

"How's my girl?" Bernie greeted Laurie with a big hug. Turning to Emma, she enveloped her in a hug as well. "Oh, you must be Emma. I have to tell you that Mac and I are so happy that this girl came into our Rob's life!"

Emma could not help but embrace the older woman back, feeling proud of her role in Laurie's upbringing. The women talked for a little while in the back of the shop. Bernie greeted most customers who came in, introducing Emma to many of them. Emma could see the look of surprise in quite a few eyes as she was introduced as Laurie's aunt.

"Did the whole town think I was older?" She smirked at Laurie. Laurie just rolled her eyes and laughed back. Bernie, Emma, and Laurie packed up pastries and coffee thermoses to take to the firehouse.

"Give my son and husband a kiss for me!" Bernie ordered in a happy voice.

"Husband?" Emma asked.

"Mac, Bernie's husband, is the fire chief in Fairfield," Laurie explained. Loaded down with goodies and goodbye hugs all around, Laurie and Emma left the shop.

They showed up with a basket of Bernie's goodies and were immediately surrounded by hungry firemen. Emma liked being swarmed by a group of very handsome men of all ages. Suddenly there were lots of helping hands, taking the pastry baskets out of Emma's hands and the coffee containers out of Laurie's hands. Rob took the coffee from Laurie and passed it to another fireman.

"Here Pete, take this. I've got to hug my woman!"

The men led Emma into the firehouse kitchen that was upstairs and she helped set up the table. She saw a well-stocked kitchen, with a large industrial stove and refrigerator. In the center of the room was a huge table that could seat the whole company.

Right then, a large, barrel-chested older man, wearing navy pants and a navy shirt with the FFD logo stenciled over the pocket, walked in from the back office and bellowed, "Where's my wife's coffee?"

Emma jumped at the loud voice behind her and whirled around. His sparkling blue eyes settled on hers, and she once again found herself enveloped in a huge hug.

"Ah darlin', you must be our Laurie's Aunt Emma." Mac was a big man, in very good shape with the good looks that made it easy to see why Rob was so handsome.

Emma loved hearing how Rob's parents referred to Laurie as theirs. She had wanted Laurie to find love and acceptance in the world, and it seemed that Fairfield held it all for her. She couldn't help but wonder if it would offer the same for her. A vision of a large, quiet, handsome police detective came into her mind. She had not spoken to him since the night at the bar and the swimming pool, but she had seen him occasionally in town. He always smiled and nodded his head at her, but she could not tell if he was interested or not.

"Earth to Emma," Laurie giggled, waving her hand in front of Emma's face. Emma blushed and looked around to see who may have seen her daydreaming. Everyone else seemed to be busy eating the last crumbs of the pastries and heading back out into the area of the firehouse that housed the fire trucks. Mac came up to her and thanked her again for bringing the treats for his men.

"Don't be a stranger!" he boomed to her as he headed back into his office. Rob walked Laurie and Emma back to their car. Emma hopped in to give them a moment of privacy, which they immediately took advantage of. Laurie hopped in, smiling.

"You look like the cat that ate a canary," Emma accused.

"Oh, it's just that Rob and I decided to throw a cookout this weekend and invite all our friends and family. That way you can meet more people."

"Is that all?" Emma asked. She knew when Laurie was up to something.

"Well, Rob mentioned how it would have made Jake crazy to see all the firemen surrounding you today. So I suggested that we see exactly how Jake will act when we have everyone over."

"Laurie Rose Dodd," Emma said in her best authoritative voice. Laurie knew that voice well. She assured Emma that they were going to have a cookout anyway, but that they just wanted to see confident Jake squirm. Emma shook her head – she knew when Laurie had her mind set on something, there was no changing it. And secretly, she would like to see how Jake would react as well.

Chapter 4

Emma was thrilled to meet with a realtor to help her find a house in Fairfield. She had talked to Laurie about wanting to buy a home, and with Laurie's emphatic blessing, she was ready to settle down. And she couldn't think of a better place to settle than near Laurie. Emma had been pinching pennies since she became Laurie's guardian at the age of eighteen. She shopped sales, bought from warehouse grocery stores, kept expenditures to a minimum, saving most of her tips from her waitressing job and most of her salary from her counseling job last year. Having to work to cover the costs of housing, living expenses, her education, and the necessities for Laurie taught Emma the value of hard work and saving.

The realtor, Linda, assuming that Emma with a job in the Fairfield school system, would want to find a house in a nice community, and was surprised to learn that Emma dreamed of buying a small, fixer-upper with some land around it. Linda was determined to find just what Emma wanted, and with help from Laurie, they poured over possibilities. They looked at several properties, but Emma had rejected them all – too expensive, too much land, too much of a fixer-upper. Finally on Saturday morning, the realtor called with another property for Emma to look at. Linda was going to be gone over the weekend, but told Emma that since the property was abandoned, she could check it out herself. Emma took down the address and told Linda that she would go look at it on Sunday since Saturday was Laurie and Rob's cookout.

She was looking forward to the cookout – Jake would be there. Each night at about ten when she went out to the hotel pool to swim, she saw his truck parked across the street. She would swim, then get out of the pool and give him a little wave as she walked back to her room. Once in her room, she peered out of the hotel window to see his truck pull away. Smiling to herself, she knew this was his way of trying to keep her safe.

Saturday afternoon Emma headed out of town to Laurie and Rob's house. They lived outside of Fairfield, off a country road with a long driveway leading to a restored two story farm house. The house was painted white with green shutters and a wraparound porch. Laurie and Rob had fallen in love with the place and had spent the last several months working on the house and landscaping.

Mature trees surrounded it. New flower gardens were planted along the front walk and around the porch. Emma made her way up the front steps, carrying her contribution to the cookout – her homemade cherry pie. Helen allowed her to use their oven that morning to bake it. To show her appreciation, she had baked two pies. One to take with her and one she left in their office with a little note, knowing Roger would love her gift.

"Come on through." She heard Laurie's voice yell from the back of the house. Emma made her way to the kitchen and set her pie down on the counter. "Emma's here," Laurie yelled out into the back yard.

"Laurie," Emma admonished, "You don't have to scream my arrival out to everyone."

"Well," Laurie grinned, "I happen to know one man out there that is very interested in your arrival."

"And who would that be?" Emma questioned, while secretly wondering if it were a gorgeous mountain of a man who just happened to be a protective policeman.

"Oh, I think you know that Jake is interested in you!" Laurie insisted.

"Gee, and I didn't think he liked *older* women," Emma shot back.

Laurie rolled her eyes, still stirring potato salad. "Yeah, well, I have just started to forgive him for that blunder!" Laurie paused in her stirring and looked at Emma, concern on her face. "I know he really feels bad about how that evening went. What *do* you think of him, Emma?"

Emma thought for a moment, then sighed. "Laurie, I've been independent for the past thirteen years. I have never had time for a relationship, and the few times I tried, they failed miserably!"

"Emma, you were always trying to be with a man who needed you to take care of him like you always take care of everyone else. You need to find someone who is strong enough to take care of you."

"Like Jake?" Emma asked. She felt conflicted about being with a man who liked to take control. On one hand it felt so nice to have someone want to look after her, but all she knew was how to do things herself.

Looking through the sliding glass door, she recognized Jake's masculine profile outside with Rob. Khaki cargo shorts slung low on his hips and a tight navy t-shirt stretched tight over his chest and arms made him easy to see and easy on the eyes. Emma yearned to run her fingers through his sandy blonde hair....especially if those arms were wrapped around her as well. The sunglasses he was wearing kept her from seeing his expression. Sighing, Emma shook her head.

"Maybe I just don't know how to be in a relationship without giving up my independence," she whispered.

Laurie enveloped her in a big hug and said, "Well for today, let's just enjoy friends!" The two women hugged and then broke apart laughing and started carrying food out to the deck.

✺

Rob and Jake had silently watched the interaction between the two women. "What do you think they are talking about?" Rob asked.

"Who the fuck knows," Jake answered, rubbing his hand over his face.

Rob glanced over at his friend, knowing that Jake was interested in Emma. "I know that Laurie is the woman she is today not just because of her mom and grandparents, but because of Emma. Emma gave up her young adulthood to provide everything she could for Laurie. Jake, I know you're interested in her, but be warned. If you hurt her, you hurt Laurie. And even though we are best friends, if you hurt Laurie, I will come after you."

Jake looked over at Rob and raised his eyebrow. "I'm interested in her, but I don't know if I have it in me to try to build a relationship, especially not with my track record of women who hightail it out of town when they find out I live with my mom," Jake said.

Rob slapped him on the back and laughed out loud. "Yeah, I hear you, man. But I think you are just shittin' yourself if you don't think she has already gotten under your skin. And seriously, Jake, Emma doesn't seem like the type to be concerned about you taking care of your mom."

Tom came up in time to hear the last of their conversation and joined Rob in a high five. Jake shook his head at his friends as they walked up to the deck to help the women with the platters.

Jake looked over at Emma as she walked across the yard. Her simple red sundress was tight on top, flared out around her hips, and came to a few inches above her knees. There was nothing overtly sexy about her apparel, but Jake easily saw he was not the only man who had eyes for her. As Emma greeted people she knew and met others for the first time, he was aware of the smile that radiated from her. Jake wondered if she could turn that radiance toward him. Scanning the group, he saw the lust-filled eyes of one of the firemen following her, he decided it was time to step up his game.

The afternoon was fun for everyone. Rob and Laurie had invited many people that Emma knew so she already felt as though she was among friends, but there were enough new people that she had the opportunity to meet. Carol and Tom were there, as well as Helen and Roger. Also there were the owners of Smokey's: Wendy, a knockout blonde, and her husband Bill, who looked like a mountain man with his bulky build and heavy beard. There were several men from the firehouse where Rob worked as well as some teachers from Laurie's school. All in all, it was a good group of friends, and Emma was thoroughly enjoying herself. Jake had been quiet for most of the evening, but he always appeared at her back whenever one of the single men came over to talk to her. At first, she thought it was just coincidence, until a latecomer came in.

"Mike!" Laurie greeted. "Come meet my aunt Emma."

Emma looked over at another good looking man approaching. *Good God, does Fairfield just grow handsome men?*

She remembered Mike was the person Laurie was going to call in to be Emma's dinner partner when Jake showed up with Brandi. She looked at him striding over. Not bad at all! Mike was tall and built, although not in the same way that Jake was. Where Jake exuded raw masculinity, Mike seemed more dapper. Funny – she always thought dapper would be her preference, but Jake was the one that made her heart beat faster as she thought about being taken by him.

Mike walked directly towards her with a huge smile on his face. As he neared, his eyes went behind her and his smile faltered as Jake appeared.

"Mike, it is nice to finally meet you," Emma said, putting her hand out toward his. He moved in closer and took her hand in his and raised it to his lips.

"The pleasure is all mine." He flashed a sexy smirk on his face.

Before she could even think of a response, she felt her hand being jerked away from Mike's lips as her arm was pulled back. Emma felt a huge presence pressed behind her back and knew who it was. As angry as she was at his presumptuous behavior, she couldn't help but notice how her traitorous body reacted. At the contact, her nipples hardened, and she felt herself clinching her legs together to ease the ache.

Mike stepped back looking over her shoulder. "Jake."

"Mike," Jake replied. The two men just stood staring each other.

Emma knew they were friends as well as co-workers, but felt as though she was in the middle of a bad spaghetti western, where two men would square off with each other in the middle of town. Rob and Tom, taking pity on her, jumped in.

"Mike, glad you could make it!" Rob exclaimed. Tom shook Mike's hand, and they walked over to the food-laden tables. Emma turned around and looked up at Jake. He was a foot taller, so she had to lean her head way back, but she was totally undaunted by this gigantic man.

She crossed her arms, cocked her hip, and began tapping her foot in irritation. "Just who do you think you are?" she hissed, not wanting to create a scene.

He looked down at her as though her question did not make any sense. "I told you that you now have someone to look after you."

"By scaring away every single man that comes around?" she glanced around to make sure no one was listening.

He looked down into her deep brown eyes. She had no idea of the effect she had on the men around. While she was just being friendly, he knew other men were plotting how to get into her pants. It was a strange feeling to not only want to protect, but to want to be around her as well. *They want a fuck buddy*, he thought, *they can go look somewhere else.*

Jake replied, "I may be friends with most of these men, but that does not mean I would trust them with my sister."

Oh, he thinks of me as a sister. Emma felt foolish for thinking that a man like Jake, who could have any woman in town, would be interested in her.

Jake saw a look of disappointment pass over her face, quickly replaced by a smile, but her smile did not reach her eyes as she stared up at him. Not able to interpret it, he found himself once again wanting to kiss that look off her face so that she would never feel disappointment again. Wanting to remove himself from further scrutiny, Jake stepped back. Emma suddenly felt cold at the loss, missing his contact.

The cookout was a success with everyone eating their fill. As evening descended, Rob started a fire in their large fire pit. Jake maneuvered his position to sit next to Emma. Casually resting his arm on the back of her chair, he was signaling to the others that she was his.

With Emma leaning forward in her chair talking, she was oblivious to the possessive position of Jake's arm or the intention behind it. Tom and Rob shared a glance and a smile.

Everyone sat around, swapping stories, and Emma enjoyed herself more than she had in years.

She realized that she had never had an evening like this one before. Eventually the conversation moved in her direction.

"Emma, have you found any houses you like?" Carol asked.

"No, not yet," Emma sighed. "I haven't looked at neighborhood homes because I would like a fixer upper on some land. Actually I am going to see a place tomorrow on my own. The realtor is out of town but said that since the house is vacant, I can go see the old Potter property." The crowd around the fire became strangely quiet, and Emma looked around in confusion.

"The Potter place?" Carol exclaimed. "That place hasn't been lived in for years... are you sure the house it still standing?" Rob, ever the fireman, noted that it may not be safe.

Mike added, "I'm sure it is not safe for you. I know of several other properties that you may want to check out. I'll be glad to offer my personal assistance."

Jake was furious. What is Mike playing at? Jake thought he had made it perfectly clear that Emma was off limits.

Several others began talking about the property, leaving Emma feeling daunted and a little defensive.

"Well, I'm still going tomorrow. Who knows, it may be perfect," she stated trying to be positive. She was determined to go no matter what.

Jake wondered why she would want an old property instead of a little house in a neighborhood or a nice apartment in town. Not about to let Emma go to an abandoned property alone, he spoke, "She won't be alone. I'll go with her."

Emma leaned back, looking over at Jake in surprise, feeling his arm on the back of her chair for the first time. "You will? You aren't going to try to talk me out of it, are you?"

Jake leaned over towards her. "It seems important to you, and I want you safe." He then leaned further and whispered in her ear, "and I want to keep taking care of you." His breath washed over her softly. Emma closed her eyes momentarily, allowing herself to wonder what it would be like to have him whisper in her ear while making love. Her eyes snapped opened, as she shook herself out of her thoughts. He thinks of me like a sister, she reminded herself. Sitting up straighter, she plastered a smile on her face.

"Thank you, Jake, but you don't have to watch out for me. I'll be fine."

He noticed that the smile, once again, did not reach her eyes. Leaning his large frame back in his seat, he kept his arm on the back of hers. "I'll pick you up at one o'clock tomorrow at the hotel," Jake said.

Emma had learned enough of Jake in the past week to know that he was not going to be deterred. "All right. I'll see you then."

 ❧

The evening was winding down with everyone was saying their goodbyes. Emma's good feelings returned. She was so grateful to have met so many friendly people. Walking arm in arm with Laurie, she headed out to her car.

"Emma, it is so good to be living close to you again," Laurie sighed.

"I know, sweetie. I feel like I have been chasing dreams for so long, but now this feels like I am home." Emma smiled back.

"So... what about Jake?" Laurie questioned. "It looked like he was doing a good job of claiming you whenever another man approached. And when Mike offered to take you around to some houses, Jake looked like he wanted to kill him."

Emma turned to Laurie. "You can stop match-making, Laurie."

"Emma, I know he comes off all macho and gruff, but he is really a good man. He is strong and loyal. Rob and Tom think the world of him."

"Oh Laurie, I don't have anything against him. Well, except the whole alpha male thing he has going on. But he told me he only thinks of me as his sister."

"He said that?" Laurie was incredulous. "Wow. I know Rob said that he hasn't been a relationship in a long time. Something about when he was younger and got really hurt. He has dated occasionally, but it seems that most women don't want to be involved with a man who has to look after his mother."

"But Laurie, that's ridiculous! He's just doing what he has to do to take care of family."

Laurie looked at her beloved aunt. "That's what you did, isn't it? With me, I mean. Emma, did you give up on relationships because of taking care of me?" Laurie's eyes shone with unshed tears.

"Oh Laurie, I never gave up anything to take care of you. We're family and that's what family does." She gazed at her niece. "And now you are taking care of me as much as I take care of you!"

"Well, I don't know Jake's whole story, but I can't believe I read him wrong. I could swear there is something there when he looks at you that is not sisterly."

"He's a gorgeous man. But hey, at least I can have a great looking hunk, who just happens to be a protective friend, right?"

Laurie and Emma hugged goodbye and Emma climbed into her little car. Laurie looked over and saw Jake sitting in his truck watching; he didn't pull out of her driveway until Emma had left. Laurie walked up to Rob who was waiting for her on the porch. He wrapped his arms around her, totally enclosing her in his hug.

"Do you think Jake just likes Emma like a sister?" she murmured into his chest.

"Hell no, girl. He may not realize what has hit him yet, but he definitely doesn't think of her as a sister!"

Laurie laughed and shook her head. "I didn't think so, but Emma does."

Rob held her back from him to he could look down into her face. He threw back his head and laughed. "Well, I guess they're both in for a surprise!"

He scooped Laurie up in his huge embrace and carried her inside. "We can finish cleaning up tomorrow woman. Let's go get naked now!"

Chapter 5

Sunday dawned a clear, sunny day and Emma found herself, anxious for Jake to arrive. It was not a date, but she had to be honest with herself – it had been a long time since she had a man take her anywhere. The six years between eighteen and twenty-four, Emma was consumed with raising Laurie, working, and taking classes – she had no time to date. If it wasn't for her boyfriend in high school, she realized that she might have been twenty-four years old and never kissed. After Laurie graduated from high school and started college classes too, there was still little time to go out. One year ago when Laurie graduated from college and moved to Fairfield to teach, was the first time Emma had been alone. She had dinner with friends, but so far no one made her heart flutter. At least not until she laid eyes on Jake.

Emma paced the small hotel room after having her morning breakfast with Helen and Roger. She tidied the small room to give her something to occupy her time. Making sure all of her clothes were put away in drawers or hanging on the rod in the back of the room, she looked around to see what else she could do. She straightened the dresser off, placing her toiletries in the top drawer. She refused to have Helen come clean for the room, wanting to take care of everything herself each day. Pulling the bed covers tighter over the comfortable bed, she began to think about what it would be like to have Jake in the bed with her. She had felt his breath caress her, wishing for his kiss. Imagining him in her bed, making love, feeling him as he pushed into her, she...

Lost in her daydreaming, Emma jumped when there was a loud knock. She opened the door, and her breath caught in her throat. Jake looked scrumptious. His hair was still wet from his shower, but mussed as though he had run his hands through it several times. What would it be like to run her own hands through his sandy blond hair? He was wearing a long sleeve, dark green t-shirt that hugged his chest like a molded skin. His jeans were slightly faded and tight enough that she could see his muscled thighs. As her eyes swept downwards, she noticed he was wearing cowboy boots. Damn, he looks good enough to eat, and he's not interested in me – just my luck.

Jake's eyes were doing their own feasting. The petite beauty in front of him took his breath away.

Her jeans were hugging her curves, her light blue top showed off her shape without revealing too much skin. Her shiny brunette hair was pulled back away from her face, allowing him focus on those deep, dark eyes that lit up when she smiled, as she was now smiling up at him.

"Ready to go, darlin'?" he drawled.

Oh hell yeah, she was ready to go.

Lifting her up into his truck, he leaned over her chest to see that she was buckled, then walked around, and got in himself. They headed out of town, toward the property they were going to look at. Jake glanced over at the beautiful woman sitting next to him.

Wanting to understand her more, he asked, "So tell me about this place. Why are you interested in it?" She was silent for a moment. Jake thought that he may have offended her.

Emma turned towards him in the cab of his truck and took a deep breath. "I grew up in a small row house in the city. It was wonderful because it was home, but it was small with no view outside the windows. There were only three bedrooms, and when Laurie was about two years old, she moved into my bedroom so that when Sarah got in later from work she wouldn't wake her up. I loved my niece, but sometimes I wished for a little more room. My favorite memories are when mom and I took Laurie and would go to the park to climb trees and run in the grass. After everyone was gone, it was too expensive for just Laurie and me, so I sold it. From the time I was eighteen until she turned eighteen, six years later, we lived in a small apartment over the restaurant where I worked part time. We shared a bedroom again. I love her and would not trade those memories for anything, but now that I can finally settle down, I want to be able to see trees from every window." She looked down at her hands in her lap. "I suppose that sounds silly, doesn't it?"

Jake glanced over at her. So much of her life had been changed when her mother and sister were killed. His own life had been unremarkable in comparison. He grew up in a nice house with a big yard with both parents. When he had been in college, getting drunk at frat parties and picking up girls, Emma had been raising a pre-teen, working thirty hours a week, and going to college part time.

"No, I don't think it sounds silly at all," he answered. Emma, grateful for his understanding, smiled. He found himself thinking that he would give anything to see that smile all the time.

With that encouragement, Emma continued. "I have been looking online at properties. The houses in town with big yards are too expensive. A couple of houses I looked at have big yards, but a lot of maintenance is required. It looks like the Potter's place is mostly wooded, private, with a small house. There weren't good pictures of the house, though. Laurie may be right – it may be disappointing."

Their destination wasn't far out of town, so in about fifteen minutes, they were turning onto a gravel driveway. Fifty yards down, the woods cleared and they could see a small house. The one story house had been painted white at one time, but the years had faded it to a greyish color. The porch ran the length of the front of the house, and an old porch swing still hung on one side. The weed covered yard had not been tended in years. What looked like an old flower pot lay on its side close to the front door. Jake looked around at the desolate surroundings. A small garage sat to the right, half hidden from the house.

He turned to Emma to express his sorrow at what he was sure was going to be her disappointment, but instead she stared at the place, beaming. The smile on her face took his breath away.

"Isn't it darling?" she exclaimed. Jake wondered if they were looking at the same house. "Come on." She threw open the door and was out of truck before Jake could unbuckle. "Let's check it out."

Jake jumped out and his long strides overtook hers. His natural protectiveness and policeman's cautiousness kicked in. "Wait. Slow down. We don't even know if it is safe."

"The realtor said that a county inspector had been out here a few months ago and said it was habitable. I'm sure it just needs a little work." Emma grabbed his hand and pulled Jake along towards the front porch.

Jake looked down at their clasped hands. Strange, he thought, how right that feels. They approached the front door, and Jake took the key from her.

"Let me go in first to check it out," he said. Jake swung the door open wide, wishing he had his revolver with him, not knowing what critters or vagrants might have taken up residence. He stepped inside, pleased to see it empty, not trashed. Emma skirted around him walking through the door. The living room encompassed most of the front of the house, with a stone fireplace at one end and built in bookshelves on either side of it. A large picture window looking out onto the front porch and yard beyond flooded the room with natural light. The hardwood floors were dusty, but in good condition.

Jake was surprised to see the solid construction of the house. He had assumed it was barely livable since Mr. Potter became a hermit in the last years of his life. Looking around, he could see the workmanship that went into the dwelling.

Emma walked over to the fireplace, smoothing her hands along the stones, already imagining her family pictures on the mantle. Turning to look out of the window, the woods surrounding the house were in plain view.

There was room on the other end for a dining table near the entrance to the kitchen, with another window facing east. Jake walked towards the kitchen, determined to scope out the rooms before Emma entered, but she followed quickly on his heels. The kitchen was simple, but roomy enough for her.

The appliances were long gone, but she could visualize where they would go. The cabinets were handmade and well crafted. Upon closer inspection, Emma was delighted to see that they did not need refinishing, just a thorough cleaning.

There was small mud room beyond the kitchen with a window and back door, leading out onto a stone patio. The mud room looked as though as a washing machine and dryer would fit in the space. Wooden pegs for hanging coats lined the opposite wall. Going back through the kitchen, they turned to head down the hall off of the living room.

There were two bedrooms, one slightly larger than the other, and one bathroom at the end of the hall. Emma peered into the bathroom. It was not large, but it held a full-sized tub. She walked into the larger bedroom that was in the back corner of the house. Looking out of the window, she could not only see the woods of the property, but the mountains in the background. Having looked at a map, she knew that the state park's land was directly behind this property.

Jake watched Emma's face as she peered out of the window. Now that he knew her history, he wondered what she thought of the view. Going back through the kitchen and out through the mud room, they walked into the back yard. Mature trees were all around and as well as the remnants of flower beds that had seen better days.

Jake was quiet, wanting to see what Emma's thoughts were. He was surprised that the house was in as good a condition as it was. It definitely needed updating and some TLC, but it was well made. He stood for a minute in the back yard, imagining Emma there. He could see her coming out of the kitchen, chasing after their children, laughing in the sunshine.

Whoa.... Their children? Where did that thought come from?

He turned around and did not see her. Walking around the corner of the house, he still did not see her. *Where did she go?*

"Emma!" he shouted, looking back and forth.

"I'm here," a distant voice cried.

"Where?"

"Up here." she called out. Jake jerked his head up, toward a rickety old ladder that stood next to the chimney. The next thing he saw was Emma's pixie face peering over the edge of the roof.

"This is great." she exclaimed. "The roof and chimney look in good condition."

Jake, trying to calm the racing of his heart, thundered, "What the hell are you doing up there? Woman, if you are not down here in two seconds, I'm coming up to get you and you're not going to like it if I have to do that." Even as he threatened, Jake eyed the dilapidated ladder, knowing it would never hold his weight. *Well, she will never know that.*

"Oh yeah? I'd like to see you get your big self up that ladder," she laughed.

"Emma, you get down here right now."

"Fine," she huffed.

Emma swung her leg over the edge of the roof, carefully stepping on the first rung of the ladder. Swinging the rest of her body around, she began to descend. Jake stood at the bottom, holding the rickety ladder steady. The third rung snapped, and Emma legs shot out from under her. Holding on with just her hands, Emma screamed out. Jake's heart pounded as he watched her flail.

"Baby, put your foot on the next one down – feel for it," he yelled. Emma got her footing and scrambled down several more rungs. By then, Jake was able to reach up and grab her by her hips, swinging her off the ladder. He whirled her around, lifted her up in his huge arms, and pressed her back against the chimney.

Leaning in, his breath right against her mouth, he choked out, "Baby, you pull a stunt like that again, and I'll take you over my knee before you can blink."

Emma stared into his blue eyes, speechless. He looks like he wants to ….

Before she could finish the thought, Jake leaned in the rest of the way and took her mouth. His kiss was forceful, and she could feel his pounding heartbeat against her chest. He slanted his mouth, gaining better access, and she opened to him. Taking the invitation, he plunged his tongue into her mouth. Her tongue tangled with his in an erotic dance that left her breathless.

Emma's breasts pressed up against his chest and he could feel their fullness, just longing for his hands. His dick stretched in his jeans and he wanted nothing more than to take her right where they were, but held himself back. He was experienced enough to know that she was lost in the kiss and he did not want her to have any regrets. Slowly, the kiss became less forceful and more of a slow exploration.

Jake leaned back, looking at Emma's kiss swollen lips.

"You got me, baby?" Jake asked, his breath mingling with hers.

Emma just stared at him wordlessly.

"Baby?" Jake said again.

Emma loved how he called her baby. "That better not be how you kiss your sister."

Jake's head snapped back, eyes wide open in surprise. "How I kiss my sister? What the hell does that mean?" he asked.

Emma realized that she spoke out loud and blushed. She tried to look down, but Jake wasn't having it. He lifted her chin with his finger so that he was able to look deep into her eyes.

"Now what do you mean about kissing my sister?"

"You said you think of me as a sister. So I thought you weren't interested."

Now it was Jake's turn to look confused. "Sister? Why the hell would you think that?"

Emma huffed, "That's what you said last night when you were chasing the other men away. You said you wouldn't trust them with your sister."

Jake hung his head for a moment and chuckled, while Emma started squirming.

"Put me down if you're going to laugh at me," she exclaimed.

Jake's eyes went back to her face that was blushing a deep red. He didn't know how, but she looked more beautiful than ever, with her hair askew, her face flushed, her breasts heaving from indignity, and a dirt smudge on her cheek.

"Darlin', there is nothing sisterly about how I feel for you, so you can get that idea right out of your head."

Emma looked up, still blushing furiously. "Oh," was the only thing she could think of to say. "Well, at least put me down." she squirmed some more.

"Hell no, darlin', you are right where I want you," he replied. Jake looked into her beautiful face and continued. "Emma girl, I noticed you at the bar before we were introduced. Now I know Brandi made that night all kinds of awkward, and as a man I hated being put in the position of trying to be a gentleman and not cause a scene when what I really wanted to do was kiss you like I just did now. Looking back, I should've shoved her away and stepped right up to you. I also know that relationships and caring for my mom haven't exactly been successful in the past, so I figured it didn't matter. But I hated like hell that you thought I was a jerk."

Emma had never heard him say so much at one time, and since she liked what he was saying, she just kept her mouth shut and her gaze on him.

"But as soon as I saw those men buzzin' around you at the cookout, I knew I had to stake my claim." At this Emma's eyebrow rose up.

"Baby, I can see you're about to get your panties in a bunch over what I just said, but I haven't felt like this in a long time, and I wanna have time to explore it without constantly fightin' men off of you." At this Jake got quiet but held her gaze.

"I've been alone for years, but not really by choice," Emma said. She gave a small smile as she looked at him, "But I'd like to see where this goes, too."

Jake dropped his gaze for a moment, then looked back up, "Well, all right then." His big speech over, he leaned back in and kissed her once more. This time is was tender, sweet and filled with promise. Emma realized that no matter which kind of kiss Jake gave her, she felt all of them right down to her core. It had been a long time since she had slept with anyone, but she found herself wondering if she was ready for Jake. She clung to him in desperation, as she kissed him, putting all the emotion she felt into the kiss.

Oh yeah, I'm ready for him.

Jake slowly lowered her to the ground, making sure her feet were securely under her before letting go. Emma gave a little moan at the loss of contact.

"Don't worry, Emma girl. I'm going to have you soon, but when we fuck, it sure isn't going to be next to the outside of a chimney in broad daylight." Emma blushed again, and Jake laughed taking her by the hand.

"Come on girl. Let's keep exploring this place."

They went back inside, checking the house over carefully. The realtor had emailed the inspector's report from a few months ago, so she knew the house was sound. She and Jake spent the afternoon talking about what she would need to fix first and what she would eventually like to do with the place. Jake liked the craftsmanship of the house. The windows and doors were straight and tight. The floors were solid.

He could see the look on her face as she measured the rooms, checked out the kitchen and bathroom, and walked around the yard. Her face showed delight, and he realized that it had been a long time since he had taken pleasure in watching someone else's joy.

They walked out on the porch and sat down on the front steps. Emma had wanted to try out the porch swing with him, but he didn't want to take a chance it would hold his weight.

Settling on the steps, they sat in companionable silence for a few minutes, allowing the afternoon sun to soak into them.

"Tell me about your mom," she asked turning her body toward his.

"Well, it was soon after my dad died that she was diagnosed with rheumatoid arthritis." He paused, looking at her. "I don't want to bore you if you know about RA."

"No, please continue," Emma replied, placing her hand on his arm. "I don't know anything about it."

"Well, RA is a bitch of a disease that affects the joints. When she was first diagnosed, I read everything I could about it. The joints become swollen, inflamed, painful, and then eventually deformed."

"Is there no cure?"

"No, although there are new drugs coming out all the time. She is on several of them and they will work for a while, and then eventually not seem to work anymore."

"Jake, I admire you so much for taking care of her. I know what it is like to put everything on hold to help take care of family. I never saw it as a sacrifice, not even a duty. It was always just done out of love."

Jake looked over at the beautiful woman sitting next to him, so closely he smelled the delicate scent of her shampoo. Their knees touched, and he found himself wanting to pull her into his lap, but the seriousness of their conversation held him back.

"She does not consider herself disabled, but she is not able to work anymore. She had been a secretary for years, but her fingers are now swollen and bent so that she cannot type or file. Sometimes if it is a bad day, she cannot grasp a phone. Some days she feels really good, but some days just getting out of bed is painful."

Jake angled his body so that they were facing each other, knowing what he was about to say could possible end the beginning of their relationship, but he knew from past experience that it needed to be said now.

Emma looked expectantly into his face, knowing that what was on Jake's mind was of utmost importance.

He looked down at Emma's small hand, still on his arm, but noticed that she was gently smoothing her fingers over his skin, as though willing him to be at ease through her touch.

"Emma, you have to understand something. We said earlier that we both wanted to see where *this* could go," pointing back and forth between each other. "But I do live at home with mom and don't know when that will end. I had an apartment of my own for a while when I first came back to town, but spent more time at her place so I just gave it up. Most women consider that to be a deal breaker," he admitted ruefully, but continued to hold her eyes.

Emma looked deeply into his baby blue eyes, knowing that in front of her was a man after her own heart. She leaned over and clasped his much larger hands in her tiny ones, holding them tightly.

"Jake, not only is that not a deal breaker with me, it makes me want to know you more than ever," she said with a smile.

Jake looked at the smile that radiated throughout him and found himself wanting that smile to greet him every day. Leaning over, he placed a gentle kiss once again upon her lips. Emma felt the strength of his emotion wrapped up in that kiss and found herself wanting it to last and last. She moved closer, and he pulled her up on his lap. Deepening the kiss, Emma knew that she was feeling more for Jake than she had ever felt for any man before.

Finally breaking off the kiss, Jake leaned back against the railing and tucked Emma into him. They sat there in the afternoon sun and continued to talk about the house.

"There are almost ten acres to the property," Emma said, looking over the reports from the realtor. "There is supposed to be a small hunting shack somewhere near the back of the property line, but I don't want to walk that far today," she added.

Jake made her promise that she would not wander around her woods without him. He glared at her, knowing how independent she was.

"No, no. Don't worry, I have no desire to get lost in the woods." she laughed.

"So what do you think?" he asked.

"I really like it. I can afford it and I feel like it is something that I can fix up, make it mine, finally have something that is all my own. It is only ten minutes away from Laurie's place and only fifteen minutes away from the high school where I will be working in the fall," Emma stated. She looked up at him questioningly. "So what do you think? I would really value your opinion."

Jake reached out and pulled her in close. As independent and self-reliant as Emma was, Jake was honored that his opinion was important to her. "It's a good place, Emma. And babe, if it puts a smile on that gorgeous face then I'm good." He leaned down for another kiss, taking her mouth in a slow, gentle kiss that affected Emma more than she wanted to admit. She knew she could fall hard for Jake and wondered if she hadn't already.

Chapter 6

The foreclosure sale went through with no hassles and Emma found herself a first time homeowner. She was so busy with the new house that the next couple of weeks seem to fly by. She and Laurie spent almost every day at the new house, cleaning, painting, and refinishing. Emma had lived in rented apartments for so many years that the idea of painting thrilled her. Choosing a soft taupe for the living and dining room, she painted one accent wall in the dining area a deep hunter green. She carried the green color scheme into the kitchen, mixing it with yellow accents. She bought new appliances and arranged to have her furniture from storage delivered. Carol came over on her days off and helped as well.

Tom, Rob, and Jake, plus several of their firefighting and police friends came on the weekends to paint the outside. Emma chose pale yellow for the house with green for the shutters. It wasn't unusual for her to look outside and see a few of the men with yellow in their hair and green all over their hands. One hot Saturday afternoon, she looked out of the kitchen window seeing Jake, Tom, and Rob all shirtless. All three were gorgeous men, but she couldn't take her eyes off of Jake's naked chest. Bulky muscles covered his arms and pecs, with just a spattering of sandy colored chest hair tapering down towards his...

"Emma, what are you staring at with your mouth hanging open?" Laurie interrupted as she and Carol walked into the room. Emma, embarrassed at having been caught gawking, snapped her jaw shut and turned around, trying to look innocent.

Carol peeking out of the window at the three Greek gods in the yards, leaned in and said, "Yummy!" All three women laughed and were unashamed to continue enjoying the view as they finished painting the rooms.

Emma desperately wanted flowers in her yard having lived for years in the city where the only flowers were at the park. Knowing that Helen loved planting, she turned to her for advice.

"What are your favorite flowers?" Helen asked. Emma, feeling silly, had to answer that she didn't know. Helen patted her hand and said, "Well then, dearie, what is your favorite color?"

At this, Emma smiled answered, "I love every color of flower!"

Helen laughed and said, "Leave everything to me – I will take care of your garden!"

Helen brought over plants in vivacious colors and began to fill up the old flower gardens around the yard and in front of the porch. This riot of color brought new life to the discarded property, creating the vision that Emma had for her home.

Helen and Roger's grandson Brad came over several afternoons to help his grandmother in the yard and to mow the grass. Emma enjoyed getting to know him and found out about the high school where she would be working. Rob's sister, Suzy, was a year younger than Brad, and she would show up on occasion as well. She was a cute, likeable girl and it didn't take Emma long to realize that Suzy had eyes for Brad. Brad tried to be nonchalant about Suzy, but his eyes would follow her whenever she was over visiting.

Emma never had such a support system before. When she thought back to all those years where she was alone raising Laurie, and then when they were struggling to finish college, it brought her to tears. Now she looked around and realized a community of friends were all helping out.

When Jake was there, he would walk by just to check up on her. He was a very touch feely boyfr... well, Emma did not know what to call him. He came to see her every day when he was not on duty and spent most of the weekends with her helping with the house.

Jake did not want her moving in until she had a security system in place. The closest neighbor was half a mile from her house. The decision about a security system quickly devolved into an argument.

Emma tried to be upfront about her finances. She had saved enough for the down payment and budgeted for appliances, but a security system was out of the question. Jake's solution was to pay for it himself, which made her uncomfortable.

"Babe, I just want you safe. You live out here, in your dream house in the woods, but you *are* a woman living alone."

In the end, Jake got his way and Emma wondered aloud if he was going to win all their arguments.

"Only the ones about your safety, Emma girl," Jake assured her, as he pulled her in for a hug, kissing the top of her head.

❧

One week later, it was move-in day. Jake wanted to be there when the movers came with her furniture, but he was called out on a case. Emma did not mind; she was so used to dealing with everything on her own, and Laurie was coming over to keep her company.

The movers backed the truck up to the front porch and began moving her furniture in. Laurie arrived just as the furniture was being taken off the truck.

"Emma, you kept the dining room set," Laurie exclaimed with a huge grin on her face. She ran over to the dining table and lovingly ran her hands over the wood.

"Oh, I couldn't get rid of some of our parent's things," Emma said, fondly remembering the many family gatherings around the table over the years. "It may be old, but it has memories for both of us. In fact, I kept almost everything except the old sofa. *That* I gladly got rid of," she laughed.

The movers hauled in the dining room and living room furniture and had started on the other furniture when Rob and Jake came over. Laurie stood on the porch directing the movers as they were coming out of the truck. Rob hopped up on the porch, grabbed her in a big kiss, making her giggle as he swung her around.

Jake, not seeing Emma, headed into the house. Hearing her voice from the bedroom, he headed down the hall. Jake walked into the room and saw that one of the movers stood too close to Emma, peering down her shirt as she looked away explaining where the bedroom furniture needed to go.

"Sure is a nice bed you've got there, lil' lady," the flirtatious mover said as he looked down at Emma. Seeing where his eyes were focused, Emma was going to put him in his place when suddenly the man was pushed backwards away from her.

"What the hell?" the man yelled as he swung around ready to fight. He looked up at Jake's furious face and immediately backed up.

Jake growled as he stalked closer to the man, but before he could land a punch, Emma stepped in.

"Jake. Calm down," she cried. "I had everything under control."

He rounded on her, his face showing his frustration. "Under control?" He was incredulous, looking at the bulky mover compared to her tiny stature.

"YES, I had everything under control," she said. The mover hurried out of the room, glad for Jake's distraction.

Jake's eyes focused on a spot on the wall over her head, as he ran his hand through his hair in frustration.

"Jake, I have told you before. I've been on my own for a very long time – I know how to take care of things myself," Emma said softly. She reached her hand up to rest it gently on his chest.

Jake sighed as he held her hand close to his heart. "And I have told you, that you now have me to look after you." He pulled her in, holding her close.

With their bodies touching from chest to knees, she took a deep breath relishing the feel of having someone hold her, caressing her back.

"I don't even know what *we* are," Emma said with her face pressed into his chest.

"You're *mine*," Jake whispered into her ear. "You just have to get used to knowing I am here for you now."

Emma, enveloped in security with Jake pressed up to her, could hear his heart beating as her head rested on his chest. She felt a peace that she had not known in a long time.

"Babe," Jake murmured. Emma raised her head back to look up into his eyes. He leaned down, his breath just a whisper over her lips. His eyes held hers for a moment before his lips moved over her lips. The kiss was gentle, the softest pressure as she savored the feel of him.

Then Emma stood on her toes for better access and grabbed onto Jake's shoulders. Jake, taking the encouragement, deepened the kiss, his tongue invading her mouth. Their tongues began a mating dance, stealing Emma's breath as found herself lifted off the floor.

Wrapping her legs around Jake's waist, she was carried back toward the bed. As he started lowering her onto the bed, the sound of movers coming down the hall with the next load of furniture could be heard. Emma jerked her head back and scrambled away from Jake, straightening her clothes as she backed up.

"Fuck!" Jake bit out. He hung his head in frustration for a few seconds and adjusted the tightness in his jeans before the movers came back in the room. He looked over at Emma, who was blushing bright red. Jake raised his eyebrow at her, but she just blushed more and shook her head. The movers left the room after carrying the dresser in and Jake simply crooked his finger at her.

Emma smiled and jumped back into Jake's arms. "I don't know if we should continue," she confessed.

"I don't give a fuck about the movers, but I know Laurie and Rob are here, so darlin', we can just put this off." Emma slid off of him and started to turn away.

"But babe?"

Emma turned back and looked up at Jake.

"This," pointing between the two of them, "is going to happen." Emma smiled shyly as Jake grabbed her hand and led her back down the hall. Glancing down at his tight jeans cupping his swollen dick, she couldn't help but wonder when *this* was going to happen. Smiling to herself, they walked into the living room to join their friends.

The house was taking shape over the next week and Emma loved it. She worked hard and fast to get the house looking like a home. Curtains were hung, knick-knacks and family mementoes were set around, and most of the moving boxes were gone. One afternoon, Laurie and Emma were in the bedroom, shaking out the new sheets and comforter that Carol had given her as a house warming gift.

"So, Em...," Laurie said while looking at the bed. Emma looked up at Laurie to see her smirking while tucking in the sheets. Emma looked at Laurie, assuming she knew what was running through Laurie's mind.

"I was just wondering if the bed has been broken in yet by you and Jake."

Emma shook her head, which only made Laurie exclaim, "Why not? What are you waiting on?"

Emma answered, "Well, we haven't had a lot of time alone." Laurie looked up and noticed that Emma had a sneaky smile on her face. "But I am hoping that will change soon – Jake is coming over tonight and for once we won't have anyone else around."

Laurie laughed. "I guess that means you want me to get lost!" Emma shared her laughter.

"Not right this minute, but yes... I want no one around tonight but Jake. And maybe, just maybe, the sheets will get broken in!"

∾

Jake, working long hours for the past two days finally got a chance to leave on time. He went home, showered, changed, and checked in on his mother. Mary smiled at her handsome son.

"Are you heading off to see that beautiful girl of yours?" she asked with a twinkle in her eyes. Jake leaned down to kiss her cheek.

"Yeah, we're finally going to have some time without everyone around," he replied. "Will you be all right?"

"Of course. In fact, I do not expect you to come back tonight!" she said with a laugh. Jake looked down at his mother in surprise. Laughing, he hugged her goodbye before he headed off to Emma's.

He stopped by the grocery store to purchase flowers and wine for her and beer for him. His mind was filled with thoughts of Emma as he was driving.

It had been a long time since he was this attracted to a woman… one that made him think of a possible future.

He, Rob, and Tom had all been players in college, not that he was proud of that fact. All three had been on the football team, big men around campus and women were plentiful. Jake occasionally had a girlfriend during his twenties, but never one lasting relationship. Less than two years ago, Tom met Carol and while they had had a rocky beginning, they fell in love and married. Rob had continued his player ways longer than either Jake or Tom, but when he laid eyes on Laurie, he was smitten. Jake was happy for his friends, but envious as well. But now…. since Emma walked into his life, he began thinking of the relationship in lasting terms. Much to his surprise, he was not nervous about those thoughts. In fact, he wanted to make sure that he could convince her of the same.

By the time Jake's musings were over, he had pulled into Emma's driveway. Her little house, spruced up with its fresh paint, stood in the clearing of the woods.

The sun was just starting to set over the top of the trees, giving everything an evening glow. The riotous flower beds were filled with splashes of color.

She did this. This was her vision and she made it happen. He looked up and saw her sitting on her porch swing. She gazed at him, her face lit up with a huge smile. She stood and he saw she was wearing a simple white sundress, showing off her tan. She took his breath away. *Tonight. Tonight, she will be mine.*

Emma ran down the front step and into Jake's arms. He chuckled as he swung her around.

"I'm glad I hadn't gotten my gifts out of the truck yet," he laughed as he set her down. He leaned in his truck, grabbing the beer and wine after handing the flowers to Emma. Jake didn't think it was possible for Emma's smile to get any bigger, but as she looked down at the flowers, she positively glowed.

"I've never gotten flowers before," she exclaimed, holding the bouquet as though it was a treasure. Jake looked at her, reminded again of how much she gave up over the years to care for Laurie and herself. Well no more, he vowed.

Arms around each other, they walked inside and Jake looked around. He was amazed at what Emma had accomplished in the three days since he had been in the house. Walking into the living room, seeing the rug on the wooden floor, blanket on the back of the couch, and curtains on the windows, he admired her decorating. Moving over to the fireplace, he looked at the framed pictures on the mantle. Emma walked up beside him waiting for his reaction. His expression was warm as he looked down at her.

"Family?" he asked.

Emma smiled and nodded. She pointed to the various pictures, explaining her life's story in the photographs.

There were pictures of her parents standing with Sarah and Emma. Sarah looked so much like Emma, he could immediately tell that they were sisters. There were pictures of the women in the family after her father died. There were the pictures of just Emma and Laurie. The faces staring back at him from the photographs all looked happy.

Jake, aware of a faraway look that flashed across Emma's face as she reminisced, understood that she would feel their loss forever. Jake pulled her in closely for a hug and once again Emma enjoyed his comforting embrace.

She looked up just as he looked down and for a moment, they simply found themselves gazing into each other's eyes.

Jake leaned down and captured Emma's lips in a kiss. His kiss was gentle at first, but as she leaned up grabbing his shoulders to pull him closer, his kiss became more urgent. He leaned down and swept Emma up in his arms. He pulled back from the kiss just long enough to give her a questioning look.

"Emma girl, you with me?" he asked. Emma smiled and nodded. That was all the encouragement he needed. Scooping her up in his arms, he carried her down the hall toward the bedroom.

Emma threw her arms around his neck to hold on, snuggling her head on his shoulder. She was ready. Whatever the night was going to hold for them, she wanted this. *I could live here in his arms forever.*

Entering the bedroom, Jake allowed her body to slide down his front until her feet reached the floor. Lips never apart, he kissed her all the while.

Like a drug, his kisses were addictive, Emma thought, needing them to live. Their tongues dueled together, flaming the passion that burned through both of them.

Jake pulled her tightly to him, their bodies pressed from chest to knee.

Emma could feel her nipples hardening as his hands roamed down her back and cupped her ass. She held onto his arms, afraid that her legs would not hold her up.

Jake snaked one hand around to her stomach, slowly moving it upwards till it cupped her full breast.

Emma heard moaning, not surprised to find that it was coming from her. As Jake kneaded her breast with one hand, the other hand gripped the straps of her dress pulling them down. Jake looked down at her full breasts spilling out of her bra.

"Goddamn girl, you are so beautiful." The dress fell to the floor leaving her in only her silk bra and matching panties. His hands went to the front snap and he wasted no time in divesting her of the scrap of lace. As her bra fell away, Jake picked her up to move her to the bed.

"I want to see all of you babe." Leaning over, he kissed her again while his hands moved down to pull off her silk panties. After sliding them slowly down her legs and tossing them to the floor, he leaned back and perused her gorgeous body. Emma blushed again, totally exposed to Jake.

"I seem to be greatly under-dressed," she said jokingly, feeling self-conscious.

"Well, I plan on taking care of that, darlin'," Jake replied, his voice husky. He pulled off his shirt tossing it into the ever-growing pile of clothes on the floor.

As he was unzipping his jeans, Emma could not help but gawk at his naked chest. Jake was powerfully built, with chiseled abs, thick muscular arms, and broad shoulders. Emma's eyes traveled down over his tight stomach muscles and the delicious V that traveled down into his pants. He pulled off his jeans, while reaching in his pocket to get out a packet and toss it on the bed. Emma couldn't help but stare.

Jake in his boxers was a sight that she would never tire of. He was without a doubt the most gorgeous man she had ever seen.

"Like what you see?"

Emma's eyes darted back up to Jake's face, seeing the smirk on his face. Emma laughed.

"Actually yes. I love what I see!" she replied.

Jake continued to hold her stare as he slid off his boxers and lowered himself on the bed. Laying on his side with Emma next to him on her back, he roamed his hands over her body exploring every delicious curve. His lips clasped over one nipple as his hands continued their exploration. He sucked one nipple fully before moving over to the other one, giving both breasts the attention they desired.

Emma felt the electric shock from her nipple directly to her core. Wanting more, she slid her hands around to his broad back, pulling him closer.

As he continued exploring her breasts with his mouth, his hand moved lower and to explore Emma's wet folds, pushing a finger inside. Emma moaned and began pushing her hips closer to him as she reached down and grasped his cock in her hand. It was impressive, silky and hard, and much larger than either of the boyfriends she had ever been with.

She suddenly felt self-conscious, realizing that she had only been with two men before and assumed that Jake had been with many women. *He has so much more experience than I do. What will he think of me? What if I don't satisfy him?*

Jake felt that she had grown still, and he moved his head from her breasts up to peer down into her face. He could see hesitation in her eyes.

"Emma girl, we can stop any time you say," he assured her, assuming she was having second thoughts.

"That's not it," she admitted. "I just don't know… I mean, it has been a long time and I …," she mumbled.

"Babe, this is going to go at your pace," he assured her. "But just know that I don't do this as a one night thing. What's going on between us, I want it and I think you want it too."

Emma looked into his eyes and nodded.

"You are the most beautiful woman I have ever seen, but more than that, babe, is your heart. You care, you give, you make everyone around you feel better just by being in your presence."

Emma was stunned. No one had ever said those words to her. Her heart was melting, but he wasn't through.

"I love bein' with you and I want you with me. This tonight, is just continuing you and me," Jake said.

Emma's insecurities fell away and she pulled him close, sealing her lips onto his in a deep kiss.

Growling, Jake moved over her, resting his weight on his arms, not wanting to crush her. Knowing his size, he wanted to make sure she was ready. He slid his hand down her body again, slowly pushing a finger into her wet pussy. Moving his finger back and forth, he revealed what elicited the most pleasure for her. Amazed at how responsive she was, he watched as she moved her hips in rhythm to his fingers. Wanting to take care of her first, he lowered his head to her breasts, sucking hard on her nipples. Sliding another finger into her wetness, he moved them around in constant motion adding pressure.

Emma felt the orgasm building as the pressure inside wound tighter and tighter. Never experiencing this with either of her previous partners, the loss of control was exhilarating.

Jake, realizing that she was close, tugged harder on her nipples as he moved his thumb over her clit, applying just enough pressure to send her over the edge.

Emma screamed out his name as the tremors overtook, feeling shattered into a million pieces.

Jake slowly pulled his fingers out after her inner muscles stopped clenching around them. He held her closely, moving his hand in slow circles over her stomach as she opened her eyes and smiled.

"You okay, baby?" he whispered just over her mouth as their breath mingled.

"Oh yeah," she whispered back, her smile lighting up her face. He leaned back in for a soft, gentle kiss. Emma kissed back, as though she needed his breath to live.

As their kiss deepened, he reached over to grab the foil packet. Leaning up, he rolled the condom onto his cock. Emma's eyes were dilated with passion as she helped guide him to her opening. Jake entered slowly, filling her a little bit at a time, allowing her to get used to his size. Emma moaned at the feeling of fullness and pressure. Jake found himself seated fully and he began to pump slowly.

"Goddamn, you're so tight," he said through gritted teeth.

"I'm sorry," Emma answered, feeling the need to apologize.

Jake moaned as he began to pump faster and faster. "Woman, that's a good thing!"

Emma was too far gone in passion to feel embarrassed at her comment. She could feel the building of tension, starting in her core and radiating out.

"Come on, babe," Jake said, knowing he was getting close and wanting her to come first. The feeling of delicious friction continued, and Emma could tell she was at the cusp of her orgasm. Jake reached down and fingered her clit, pushing her over the edge.

Emma's orgasm exploded, taking her whole body in its wake. She was barely aware of Jake, when he tensed, his jaw and neck muscles straining, as he came right after she did. Jake dropped down onto Emma, trying not to crush her. Emma did not seem to mind, as she slowly moved her hands over his sweat slicked back.

Jake raised up on his arms, peering down into her face. Emma looked up smiling, and moved her hands to cup his face. He brought his lips back to hers in a slow, languid kiss. He rolled to the side, moving his weight off of her. He got up and stalked to the bathroom to dispose of the condom. Striding back to the bed, he noticed that she had moved under the covers. Raising his eyebrows, he leaned down and snatched the sheet back.

"Don't want you to hide that beautiful body, Emma girl," he said. He lay back down on the bed gathering her into his arms. Cuddling in bed for a while, they allowed the feeling of contentment to wash over them.

Emma's stomach growled, and she giggled. "I think I need to go to the kitchen and fix some dinner," she said.

Jake could have stayed in bed for round two, but wanted Emma to go at her pace. Getting up, she threw on his shirt and her panties before leaving the room. Jake smacked her on the ass as she passed him in the bedroom. Squealing, she turned around, attempting a pissed off look.

"That look won't work on me," he laughed. "And I like you in my shirt," he added. Emma smiled and headed down the hall, sweeping her tresses into a messy bun. A few minutes later Jake walked into the kitchen, leaned against the door-frame and watched Emma flitting around the room. She was like a tiny whirlwind, moving around as she threw together a quick meal. The chicken was already baked and it took little time to sauté the vegetables.

Jake's shirt was huge on her and yet he could clearly see her nipples poking through the material. Every time she raised her arms to reach for some-thing high, his shirt lifted enough to show the bottom of her perfect ass. He shifted uncomfortably as he felt his blood running back to his dick again.

Glancing over her shoulder she saw him stand-ing there, looking like an Adonis. Standing still for the first time since entering the kitchen, she stared at his masculine perfection. Her eyes took in all of him, from his sex tousled hair, down his defined six pack, his low slung jeans hanging on trim hips, all the way down to his sexy bare toes.

Smirking, Jake asked, "Something I can do for you, baby?"

Jolted out of her thoughts, Emma blinked and snapped her mouth shut. Huffing, she turned to pull the hot rolls out of the oven. "Well, you can stand there looking delicious enough to eat... or you can set the table and we'll feast on this meal for now."

Laughing, Jake took the plates and silverware off of the counter and set the table. For the rest of the evening they ate, talked, watched TV, then headed back to bed for round two and three before falling into an exhausted sleep.

Waking early the next morning, Jake watched Emma sleeping on her side. Her hair fanned out on the pillow behind her with just a few wisps falling across her face. One hand tucked under her head, she made the slightest noises as she slept. The sheet had fallen off her shoulders, and he could see the curve of her full breast. She was the most beautiful woman he had ever seen. A feeling of contentment overcame him.

Emma's eyes fluttered open, first in confusion, then a slow smile came across her face.

"I could wake up every mornin' in your arms and be a happy man," Jake admitted.

Emma's eyes grew wide at this confession, her smile even brighter. "And I could do the same," she agreed shyly.

Jake's arm snaked around her and pulled her tighter. They lay flush together, and she felt his cock nudging her.

Emma raised her eyebrows. "Ready again?" she asked with a chuckle.

"Oh baby, I am always ready for you," he claimed as he leaned in for another toe curling kiss. Round four came before they made it to breakfast.

Chapter 7

A few days later, Tom, Jake and Mike were sitting at their desks discussing a new case they were working on. Like many small towns, the citizens of Fairfield enjoyed a low crime rate for a number of years, but now that it was a growing city, crime was on the increase. Drug use among teenagers was on the rise, and last night the police busted a party where various drug paraphernalia had been confiscated. Arresting the teen users was only part of the solution but they needed to get at the source of the drugs coming into their county. So far, their leads had resulted in dead ends. The drug runners and dealers stayed one step ahead of the police, and the detectives were increasingly frustrated. Mike had been trying to compare their data to some of the surrounding counties to see if he could find correlations. Tom and Jake were reviewing the evidence from the scene of last night's party.

Mike looked at his watch and stood. "All right guys, I'm heading out. Got a date and don't want to be late!" he joked. He looked down at Tom and Jake still sitting at their desks. "Don't know what you two are waiting on – not with your women at home," he said over his shoulder as he left their office. Tom tossed another file on his desk in frustration.

"Jake, I'm done, man. I can't look at this shit anymore today." Smiling, he added, "And I've got a hot wife at home who is off work today, just waiting for me."

"Don't rub it in, Tom." Jake answered back, also tossing his file on his desk.

"Well, don't you have a sweet little brunette waiting for you?" Tom asked. "How are things going with you and Emma?"

Jake, closed mouthed as usual, just said, "They're goin'."

Seeing the little smile on Jake's face, Tom continued, "Yeah, I hear you. But I also think that sweet girl is the best thing to come your way."

A slow smile spread across Jake's face as he looked up at his friend. "Don't I know it!" he replied.

"So why don't you make it official?" Tom asked.

Surprised, Jake looked at his longtime friend. "We've only been together a few weeks."

"Hey, I knew the minute I met Carol, she was it for me. I couldn't wait to get a ring on that finger," Tom replied.

Jake nodded, remembering how he made fun of Tom being pussy whipped so soon after meeting Carol, but now he completely understood. "Yeah, I remember," Jake answered. "But I don't want to scare her off. I want to make sure that this is right for both of us." He looked back at Tom and grinned. "But I'm not letting her get away."

Rising from their chairs, the two friends fist bumped and headed out of the station, each anxious to get to the women awaiting them.

A few days later, rising before dawn, Emma made her way to the front porch swing with her cup of coffee. Always a morning person, this was her favorite time of day. Dawn. When the day was new and held infinite possibilities. Skimming the tops of the trees on the east side of her yard, the sun's light was painting the dark sky a softer shade of blue. Continuing to watch the sun rise, the sky became a kaleidoscope, as reds, yellows, pinks, blues and oranges all clashed with each other. A slight morning mist floating across her yard began to dissolve.

The only sounds Emma heard was the squeaking porch swing and birds flitting around the bird feeders. Looking at the bird feeders, Emma smiled at the memory of Jake's gift. One morning, he drove up to her house bearing gifts. A bird feeder, birdbath, and different types of bird seed. Running into the yard to greet him, she questioned his gift. His simple explanation: she had once mentioned that when she lived in her apartment she would feed the pigeons and she always wished to be able to feed song birds.

That was Jake. He listened. He remembered. He acted.

The squawking of birds pulled her out of her musings. Glancing across her yard, she saw a small furry creature slowly making its way toward the birdbath. Curious, she walked down the porch steps to get a better look. A small cat, fur matted, mewed in her yard, staring at her with huge eyes. It did not appear to be afraid of her as she approached it slowly. Carefully scooping it up, she was surprised that it did not attempt to scratch her or escape.

Rubbing its ears, she heard the distinct sound of purring. "Oh baby, are you lost? Are you hungry?" Taking the stray inside, she found some chicken and rice for him to eat. Gobbling the food, the cat walked into her living room finding a sun spot, then proceeded to take a bath.

"Well, you have certainly made yourself at home."

Later that day, Emma purchased cat food and made an appointment with the closest veterinarian. Once at home, she walked in and was immediately greeted by the cat circling her legs begging for attention. Giving him some real cat food, he once again gobbled it up. "A few more meals like this and your ribs won't show anymore."

That evening Jake was on duty so Emma was alone in her bed. It did not take the cat long to discover that its owner slept in a warm soft bed. Making itself even more at home, the cat quickly snuggled on the pillow next to Emma, sleeping soundly through the night.

The next morning as Emma sat on her porch swing, watching the dawn, listening to the birds, and seeing her cat play on the porch, she realized something. *I'm home.*

∾

School started for Emma in late August. She met her co-workers, settling into her role as a high school counselor. The school was similar to her last one, and she found that teenagers were much the same everywhere. The other counselor was an older gentleman, soon to retire, but Emma found that the students respected him and he was treated with a grandfatherly respect. Students quickly flocked to her as well. Whether it was school problems, home problems, college applications, or just to talk, she loved all aspects of her job.

Jake made his presence known during the first couple of weeks, dropping by to see her at the end of the school day when he was in the area. Emma grinned to herself – she knew Jake well enough by this time to know he was publically staking his claim.

Emma, sitting in her office, looked over the most recent grades of some of her students. As she tried to familiarize herself with the students, she came across Brad's grades. A significant drop in his grades from last year occurred, and she wondered what was going on. She called for him to see her toward the end of the day and when he came in he greeted her warmly. Sitting for a few minutes, they enjoyed chatting about her house, his part time job, and family.

"Brad, you probably are wondering why I wanted to see you," Emma said with a smile.

Brad grinned back and answered, "Yeah. My grades, right?"

"Since I am new this year, it has taken me a while to get around to all my students, and I really just realized how your grades have slipped."

Brad smiled a charming smile and easily replied, "Oh, I have just been working too many hours down at the store."

Emma did not say anything for a minute, deciding to see what else Brad would say. His smile began to slip away as he looked anywhere in the room but in her eyes. Emma knew when she was being fed a line.

"Brad, I think there is more to it than that. Your grades are not the only ones slipping. I am noticing that a few members on the football team grades are slipping." Again, Emma waited to see what Brad's response would be. He began to squirm uncomfortably in the chair. At this point, Emma became concerned.

"Brad, I was going to talk to the coach tomorrow to see if he can tell me why some of his boys are starting to fail, but I was really hoping you could give me some insight first."

"Honest, I don't know why my grades are so poor, Ms. Dodd," Brad answered, "but please don't talk to the coach. I'll talk to the boys, and we'll start working harder. I'm sure that's all it is — just too much homework, not enough time to get it all done with practice and jobs. It's nothing else. You don't want to go stirring up trouble looking for something else!"

Emma, raised her eyebrows. "I wasn't looking for something else, Brad," she said slowly, perusing him carefully. "But you are making me concerned right now."

Brad looked into her eyes with a desperation she had not seen before. All of Emma's senses were on high alert. She sensed Brad was lying and hiding something. Maybe it was just the coach's wrath, she thought.

"Okay, well, for now just see if you can cut back on your shop hours and if you need some after-school tutoring in your harder classes, just let me know."

Brad let out his breath and looked up with a smile, one that did not reach his eyes. "Sure thing, Ms. Dodd. I'll work harder, and the grades will come up, I promise."

Brad left her office and Emma spent the next hour looking at the grade history of many of the students. New to the job, she didn't have the knowledge of their grades without looking up each one. Closing her office door, she headed down to the gym to see the coach. The football coach was also the wrestling coach, so she knew most of the boys would be continuing their sports into the winter.

"Ted?" she called into the PE teacher's room. He was packing up his bag.

"Hey, Emma," he greeted. Ted was a big man, probably very good looking in his younger days and was aging well. He was in his early forties, divorced, with dark hair that was sprinkled with some gray. He kept in shape by working out with "his boys" as he liked to call them. His personality made him popular among the students. Ted greeted everyone with a loud voice and a friendly smile. "Whatcha need, Lil'Bit?" he called out.

Emma grinned. "Ted, you watched too much Little House on the Prairie, when you were younger!" referring to the nickname he bestowed on her.

"Just call em like I see em," he laughed, looking her up and down, his eyes settling back on hers.

Emma explained she needed to see him about some of his player's grades and her concerns.

The smile left Ted's face. He was very protective of his boys. "Well, I've got to head out to practice now. We won't be done till about five thirty."

"Can I talk to you tomorrow then?" Emma asked.

"Sure," Ted answered. Ted hesitated for just a second then said "How about we grab a bite of dinner after practice, and we can talk then?"

Emma hesitated. She really wanted to get his insight on the students they both cared about, but found herself wondering what Jake would think about her having dinner with another man. That's ridiculous, she chastised herself. It was a working dinner, not a date, so Jake would have no reason to be concerned. And if she and Ted talked tonight, she would sleep better knowing there would be a plan to help the students.

"Sure," Emma said. "We can meet at the diner about six o'clock?"

"Sounds like a date," Ted boomed as he escorted her out of the door.

Emma debated as to whether or not she should tell Jake about meeting with Ted. On one hand she hated to think that she had to report to him, but on the other hand she could see that it could be misconstrued. Deciding to at least let him know what she was doing, she simply texted him.

Have teacher mtg at diner tonight. Talk to you later.

Knowing he was working and wouldn't answer back for a while, she decided to drive downtown to accomplish some errands before meeting with Ted. Walking out to her car, she saw Brad and a couple of boys talking together. They all turned their heads, looking her way as she got to her car. Their expressions did not make her nervous, but looked guilty as though they had been caught talking about her. She pushed those thoughts out of her mind and headed off to the stores.

A couple of hours later, Emma was sitting in a booth at the diner waiting for Ted. The diner was an updated version of an old soda shop. A counter running along the side of the room allowed customers to sit on high stools. The other side of the room had booths and tables. A plump waitress came over to take Emma's order. She explained that she was waiting on someone and would order when they arrived.

Ted finally came in, belting out his greetings to everyone around. Hugely popular in the small town where everyone loved high school sports, he was considered a hometown character. Emma couldn't help but grin at him, enjoying his popularity. Ted plopped himself down in the booth across from her, as the waitress came back over to take their orders.

Waiting for their food, Emma took several papers out of her briefcase and gave them to Ted. "As you can see, there are at least four of your starting seniors whose grades are plummeting. They will still be academically eligible to play, but it is not like these boys to do so poorly."

Ted looked over the grade sheets carefully, keeping his expression neutral. "You seem to be implying that something is going on besides just not doing their work," he stated.

"Ted I don't know what is going on. But I would like to ask that each of these boys stay with me for thirty minutes of tutoring after school each day before practice. That way I can make sure to help them keep up with their homework and maybe find out what is going on with them."

Ted seemed hesitant at first, which Emma found irritating. *Why was he hesitating? Was there something that he knew?*

"Ted, if you are worried about them missing practice, I promise the tutoring won't cut into practice time. But you have to admit that if you don't agree and they become academically ineligible to play, you and they lose?"

Faced with that possibility, Ted agreed that her plan was sound. Smiling back at Emma, he was just about to ask her for drinks after dinner. Before he could say anything, the broad smile on his face faltered as he looked over Emma's shoulder.

"Emma," said an angry voice next to her, pulling her out of her thoughts. Emma jumped in her chair, swinging her head around, knowing whose voice she was hearing. Seeing Jake always brought a smile to her face, but she instantly knew he was not happy.

"Jake, hey. Did you get my message?" she asked, hoping Jake was not caught unaware.

"Got a text, babe, about a school meeting," he said with his eyes raised at Ted.

Ted, seeming to be glad for the interruption, greeted Jake with a smile. "Jake, good to see you. Miss Emma needed to talk to me so I thought I would take the opportunity to take the lovely lady out to dinner."

Emma swung her head around to Ted, her mouth hanging open. "This is not a date," she stammered. "We were talking about some students I am concerned about."

Jake, realizing that Emma had misinterpreted Ted's intent, sat down next to her determined to make it very clear to Ted just who Emma belonged to. As he sat next to her in the booth, he wrapped his arm around her shoulders and pulled her in closely.

At this, Ted then raised his eyebrows at them. "Well, I see I have missed the first opportunity," he said.

Emma, feeling as though she was in the middle of a pissing contest, grew angry. "Ted, I wanted to present my idea about a tutoring session for your boys; that is all this is. Do you agree that it is a good idea and will you support me?"

Ted looked contrite and said apologetically, "Absolutely, Ms. Dodd. I think it's a great idea. Sorry if I offended you."

Since they had already finished their meal and paid, he stood and looked down at them. "Jake," he said looking straight into Jake's eyes. "Hope you know what you have there?"

Jake just gave a head nod.

"Ms. Dodd, I will see you tomorrow and I'll let my boys know to report to you after school." He couldn't resist giving her a wink as he turned to leave.

Jake growled behind Ted's back, but it turned into a grunt as Emma's elbow jabbed into his side.

"Let me out," Emma said, pushing against Jake who had her pinned in the booth. Pushing against him was as effective as pushing against a large tree.

Jake just looked down at her. "Not doin' it babe."

"Jake if you don't move I am going to scream," she said, in truth knowing she would never do that.

"Darlin', I get you're pissed, but I am not apologizin' for wantin' to make sure everyone knows who you belong to." Jake could feel the tension rolling off of Emma. "Don't go getting all independent on me. I know you're a competent woman, but I want to take care of you. And we are an *us*," he said pointing back and forth between them.

"I know we are together, but Ted an-," Emma started to explain, but Jake jumped in.

"Emma girl, I'm tellin' you I have known Ted for years. He loves football and he loves women. Couldn't keep his dick in his pants when he was married, so he's not married anymore. And there was no way, he was just here for a talk."

Emma's shoulders slumped. Why did men have to be so complicated? They always thought that women were, but it was men who she couldn't figure out. She knew Jake was upset, but really did not know what to say. He pulled her in for a hug, resting his chin on her head.

"Jake, I feel like I should apologize because you're upset, but honestly, I didn't do anything wrong."

Jake felt Emma's breathing hitch, as though she was holding back tears. "Come on, sweetheart, let's get out of here."

Emma allowed Jake to lead her out of the diner and he lifted her up into his truck.

Once settled, Jake turned to her. "You don't owe me an apology – you're right, you did nothin' wrong. And you need to know, babe, I wasn't checkin' up on you. I was just going to drop by to say hello, but when I saw Ted leaning towards you, I knew he was makin' a play." Emma sat quietly. "You don't owe me any explanation, but what's goin' on with Ted's players?" he continued.

"I can't discuss students, Jake, but I will say that I have some academic concerns and wanted to discuss a helpful idea with him. He suggested we meet for dinner."

"Yeah, I got that," he said frowning. Emma huffed and crossed her arms in front of her defiantly. Jake couldn't help but notice that not only was she cute when angry, her arms had pushed up her breasts and suddenly any thoughts of Ted flew out of his mind. In fact, the only thing that was on his mind at the moment was getting her back to her house, where he intended to make sure she knew who she belonged to.

Reminding him she had driven to the diner, Emma turned toward the door of the truck.

"I'll follow you home," he told her. She rolled her eyes, and reached for the door handle but Jake stopped her. "Emma girl, no woman of mine is gettin' out of my truck unassisted." When Emma started to protest, he just reminded her, "My momma raised me better than that."

Hopping down, he walked around to her side. Opening the door, reaching in and lifted her out, he set her down carefully on the pavement. Leaning in, his massive body surrounded her as his hands continued to span her tiny waist.

Emma's face was pressed against his chest as he enveloped her and she breathed him in. Lifting her head back to stare into the eyes that completely captured her, she reached her arms around and pulled him closer.

Leaning down, Jake placed a gentle kiss on the corner of her mouth, his breath mingling with hers. Minutes later, he slowly pulled back and Emma felt the cool air as she was separated from him. Wrapping his powerful arm around her shoulder, he walked her over to her car. "Drive safe, baby. I'll be right behind you."

Driving home, Emma wondered about their relationship. Jake was not the first man she had been involved with, but there was never time for a long term relationship. Life always got in the way. She had been on her own for so long – it was all she knew. But how nice it felt to have a gorgeous, sexy, caring man wanting to look after her. Emma smiled to herself as she drove down the road, looking in the rear view mirror and seeing Jake right behind her.

Balance, that's what I need. Balance between being cared for and not losing myself in the process.

Satisfied with her solution, she parked and grabbed the shopping bags out of the back seat. Before she could close the car door, Jake scooped her up in a fireman's hold, carrying her up to her front door. Using his spare key, he quickly opened the door then shut it behind them.

Before Emma could get out a word, he slid her body down his front, slamming his mouth onto hers. This kiss was hard, demanding, controlling. All thoughts of telling Jake to back off fell away as his mouth plundered hers. Reaching up, she grasped his face to pull him closer.

Jake needed no more encouragement. He backed her up to the front door, lifting her in his arms. Emma wrapped her legs around his waist, and he grasped her ass with one hand.

Continued to kiss her, Jake moved his other hand to the front of her shirt pushing it up to expose her bra. Pulling down the cups, he released her breasts bringing them to his mouth. He sucked one nipple, tugging the hard point deep into his mouth, and then slightly bit down.

Emma moaned, the connection sparking through her from her breasts directly down to her core. Squirming, she tried to rub her throbbing pussy against his cock, straining in his jeans.

"More," she panted.

Jake growled his response as he pushed his hand up her skirt and grabbed her panties. Ripping her panties with one pull, he tossed them to the side. Continuing to kiss her senseless, he undid his jeans and pushed them down to his knees.

"Spread," he ordered, and Emma spread her legs as wide as she could, continuing to wrap them tightly around his waist. Fingering her pussy, he was thrilled to find it already wet for him.

"Soaked, baby," he acknowledged, but Emma already knew she was ready for him.

"Now Jake. Please now," she moaned, digging her fingernails into his shoulders.

Jake obliged, pushing his cock fully into her. He began to thrust, pounding her against the door as he took her, marking her, making her his.

Emma felt the pressure building and knew her orgasm was coming quickly. Eyes shut tight, she gave over to the complete feeling of being thoroughly fucked and thoroughly cared for at the same time. Emma screamed Jake's name as her inner muscles contracted strongly, pulling at his straining cock. Jake continued to thrust several more times before he felt himself come deep inside of her, pulsating until he was emptied.

It took a minute for his heartbeat to slow and he lowered his head to capture her lips again in a soul searing kiss. Letting Emma slide down to the floor, he held her close until her legs were steady. Pulling out of her, he looked down as their mixed fluids ran down her leg. Emma, aware of his eyes on her, looked down at herself as well.

Realization washed over Jake. "Oh God, Emma, I'm so sorry," he exclaimed. Emma looked at him questioningly, not understanding his outburst.

"I forgot a condom," he said looking into her eyes. "I promise I've never done that before. I'm clean, I swear."

Emma, wide eyed, nodded. "I trust you Jake. I'm clean too. I haven't been with anyone before you in years."

Jake reached his hand and cupped her cheek. "But baby, what about protection? No matter what happens, baby, I'll...," Emma put her fingers to his mouth, effectively shushing him.

She smiled up at him, leaning her face into his hand. "It's okay, Jake. I'm on the pill to regulate my periods. It's all good."

Jake leaned in closer to her so that their bodies were pressed together from chest to knee. "Yeah, it's all good. Very good," he replied. "In fact, it's never been better. It's never felt like that for me, Emma girl. That was amazing."

Just then, something furry rubbed against Jake legs. Jumping back, stumbling over his pants, he began to fall pulling Emma down on top of him. A yowling sound screeched through the room, causing Jake to scramble up over her to get to his revolver.

Emma, gasping and red faced from laughing, was still lying partially naked on the floor.

Jake getting to an ungraceful stand, stared at a scrawny yellow cat glaring up at him. "What the fuck is that?" he roared, attempting to pull his pants up.

The cat calmly walked over to Emma. She reached out her hand to pet him, explaining, "I found a stray in my yard and adopted him." Stifling her giggles, she attempted to stand as Jake assisted her from the floor.

"Bloody hell, babe. You could've warned me," Jake bit out, fastening his pants.

"Honey, why are you putting your pants back on? Surely you're not done with me yet are you?" Emma said looking up into his still shocked face.

Jake's eyes moved from the cat back up to hers. "Babe, a man does not want his dick hanging down with anything that's got claws like that," he stated as a fact.

Laughing again, Emma tried to placate him. "Jake, he won't hurt you. He slept with me last night and was perfect."

Swinging his gaze back to her, Jake stated emphatically, "Emma girl. That cat and I are not sharing a bed. Not tonight. Not ever. The cat stays out of the bedroom."

Walking over, placing her hand over his heart, she looked up into his face. Standing on her toes, pulling his face down toward her, she placed a gentle kiss on his lips. "Okay, baby. You're the only male in my bedroom."

Satisfied, Jake leaned in to deepen the kiss. Jake picked her up again and walked to the bathroom, leaning into the shower stall to turn on the water.

Emma, confused, said, "Jake, I am perfectly able to take a shower myself."

Jake slowly lowered her to the ground, but kept his arms around her, holding her tightly. "Baby, there are lots of things you *can* do by yourself, but let me do this. Let me take care of you."

He slowly peeled off her clothes. When the water was warm, he moved her under the spray as he quickly divested himself of his clothes. Stepping into the shower, he grabbed the shower gel. Lathering her back, Jake made his way down to her luscious ass where he spent a great deal of time washing.

Emma, giggled, "Is that the only place you plan on getting clean?"

"Oh Emma girl, I plan on giving *all* of you this attention," Jake answered, moving his hand between her legs.

Moaning, Emma leaned against him as he continued his ministrations. Jake turned her around and began to lather her breasts. After thoroughly washing every inch of her body, he began washing her hair. Massaging her scalp as he washed, Emma could not remember ever being so relaxed and pampered.

Smiling, she faced him squirting the shower gel in her hands saying, "Now, it's your turn." She began to wash his chest, marveling at the expanse of muscles. She worked her way up to his shoulders and around to his back, slowing sliding her hands down to his ass. Looking over his shoulder, he smirked down at her.

"I just never knew how fun this could be!" She moved around again so that she was facing him, gliding her hands down to his cock. Emma began to stroke his manhood, moving her hands up and down his length. Her small hands could not grasp all of him, but the sensations created had Jake throwing his head back and groaning.

He grabbed Emma under her arms, lifting her up and turning so that the spray of water was hitting him on his back. Pressing her against the shower wall, he slammed his lips onto hers. His tongue swept into her mouth as Emma's tangled with his. She wrapped her legs around him, moaning as he sucked on her tongue and nipped at her bottom lip.

No longer worrying about a condom, Jake couldn't wait to feel skin on skin again. He checked her readiness with his finger and then pushed his thick cock all the way in, pressing her back against the wall.

"Can you take it, baby?"

"Oh god, Jake, yesssss!" she screamed. Jake pounded inside her, over and over until he felt her muscles contract around his cock. She threw her head back, eyes tightly closed, and face strained as the orgasm washed over her. Jake immediately pushed harder one more time and felt himself explode inside of her, his seed spilling deep. Both panting, he held her tightly as their breathing slowed.

Jake looked deep into her sparkling eyes, satisfied with the smile on her face. Leaning in, he kissed her softly before lowering her down. Surprised that the water was still warm, he turned her towards the spray once again, washing between her legs.

Stepping out, he wrapped her in a towel, patting her dry. Emma moved to the bedroom where she put on his t-shirt as he dried himself. Jake walked into the bedroom to see Emma folding the covers down.

"Can you stay tonight?" she asked hopefully. Not wanting him to feel pressured, she quickly added, "But if you have to go home to check on your mom, that is fine."

Jake walked over, looked down at her beauty, and brought his hands up to cup her lovely face. "I checked on mom earlier. She's fine. And babe? There is no where I'd rather be than right here with you tonight."

Smiling up at the face that had crept into all of her dreams, she took his hand pulling him down with her. They curled together in bed, Jake pulling Emma tight against him.

I've found the one, I just know it. Emma went to sleep with a smile on her face.

I've found the one, I'm gonna cherish her. Jake slept better than he had in years.

Chapter 8

E mma decided to throw a party, thanking all of her friends for helping her get moved in and working on her house. An outdoor fall party would be perfect, complete with barbeque, beer, and a fire pit in her backyard for smores and snuggling. The Saturday of the event dawned bright and clear, the sun shining over the woods, filling the air with the crisp coolness so welcome by the end of summer. Emma cleaned all day and Laurie came over to help with the food. Tom and Jake manned the barbeque, Rob took care of the large fire pit, along with some of the other firefighters, and Carol was in charge of the smores. Helen, Roger, Wendy, Bill and Brad came and Emma watched Brad finally hanging out with Suzy in public. Mac and Bernadette arrived, bringing Mary with them since Jake had gotten there early. Several of the firefighters brought dates as well as several of Emma's co-workers.

Jake looked over when Ted showed up, but stopped scowling when he saw that Ted had a date. Emma rolled her eyes at him until another teacher came, bringing Brandi. She hadn't seen Brandi since that first night at the bar. Even knowing Jake had no desire to be around Brandi, she couldn't help but feel a little jealous. Brandi, oblivious as ever, made the rounds to all the single men. Emma relaxed once it became apparent Brandi had the good sense to stay away from the claimed men and Emma made sure that everyone knew that Jake was hers. Mike was there, along with some other people from the police force.

Emma was glad she had bought enough food although it helped that many of the guests brought dishes, desserts, or beer.

"Do you have enough, dear?" Mary asked, walking back into the kitchen. Emma looked up and smiled at Mary as she walked over to hug her. She pulled out a chair and helped Mary to sit. "Don't fuss over me" Mary ordered with a smile.

Emma admired Mary so much, knowing that Mary was in pain most of the time but never complained. "I'm not fussing," Emma said. "Just being a good hostess like my momma taught me."

Mary laughed, loving the beautiful woman who had captured her son's heart. Jake walked in, looking at his mother and Emma laughing and his heart warmed at the sight of the two women that meant the most to him enjoying each other's company. Walking all the way into the room, he stooped to kiss his mother's cheek before continuing over to the counter to wrap his arms around Emma.

"Just came back in to get some more hamburgers, doll," he said, reaching around Emma to grab the plate of meat. "Everything is almost ready so I wanted to make sure my two favorite women were ready as well."

Emma grabbed a couple of more dishes and handed a small platter to Mary to carry out. Mary smiled as the made her way out into the back yard.

Jake looked at Emma's face. "How did you know that would make her happy?" he asked in amazement.

Reaching to cup his face in her hand, Emma smiled. "Everyone wants to feel useful, Jake. Your mom needs help with so many things, but she doesn't want to feel helpless. So even something as simple as me giving her a dish to take out, makes her feel as though she is contributing."

Jake stared in wonderment at the woman in front of him, not believing that he had the good fortune to be able to call her his own. "Emma darlin', just want to put it out there... I am falling for you," he told her softly.

"Jake, just putting it out there.... I already have," she whispered back. Jake's eyes grew wide but before he could respond, Emma grabbed her platter and headed out to the yard.

His eyes followed her as Emma walked in front of him. Lordy, he would never get tired of looking at that ass, cupped just perfectly in her tight skinny jeans. Her light green sweater was slightly large and hung off of one shoulder. *God, how can a sweater that is so big, look so goddamn sexy and show off her tits?* Growling, Jake grabbed the next platter and followed her out.

The dinner had been consumed, games had been played, and now the guests sat around the fire pit relaxing in the comfort of good food and good company. The sparks from the fire rose in the air as the wood crackled and snapped. Everyone's faces were illuminated only by the firelight, casting shadows all about them.

Emma's cat, who she simply named Mister, walked around sneaking tidbits from the plates, then sat by the fire watching the sparks. Sitting on a blanket, Emma snuggled up against Jake's chest. The fire gave off heat, but she was aware that the heat coming from Jake's body was providing all the warmth that she needed. She wiggled, wanting to burrow down deeper in his arms. Jake chuckled and wrapped his mighty arms around her tighter.

Leaning down to whisper in her ear, "You warm enough, babe?" Emma sighed in response and leaned back closer.

Mike looked around at her yard and nodded toward Emma. "This is a great place, Emma. You've really done a nice job with it," he said.

Emma, full of pride, smiled back. "I can't believe it is all mine. It feels so good to finally put down roots and know that when I drive down the driveway, I'm coming to *my* home. I seem to remember when some of you couldn't believe that I was actually going to even look at this place."

"How many acres do you have?" asked one of their friends.

"About ten acres, but it feels like more. There is a small part of the river that backs to the property and beyond that is the state park, so I have no neighbors back there," she replied.

"Have you walked it all yet?" Ted asked.

"No, but I was thinking that I needed to do that soon. Mike keeps scaring me with stories about critters around in the woods so I didn't want to go by myself." she answered. "There is supposed to be a tiny hunter's shack near the river, but I haven't seen it yet. I was thinking of walking down there tomorrow."

Mike looked across the fire at her. "Emma, I don't think it would be safe to go by yourself and I know Jake is on duty tomorrow."

Jake, walking back from the house having run in to get more beer, agreed. "Babe, wait a little longer until we can go together."

"I'm not helpless," Emma huffed.

Laurie, leaning back on Rob's chest spoke up. "I could go tomorrow with you."

Emma smiled at her niece. "Perfect, it's a date!"

The conversation continued to flow until the guests began to leave. Emma hugged them all, feeling for the first time in her life she was really home. Home with friends, family, and a house that welcomed them all.

Jake was finishing the cleanup from the party, when he looked over at Emma's face. He saw exhaustion mixed with her contented smile. He left the room for a few minutes and when he came back, took her by the hand and led her down the hall to the bathroom. Emma looked in and was shocked at what she saw. The tub was full of bubbles, and candles were lit on the bathroom counter. She turned around, looking up into his baby blues, that were sparkling in the candlelight.

"Baby, you're about to drop on your feet. Strip off, climb in that tub, and have a good relaxing soak."

Emma, overwhelmed that he did this simple and yet poignant act for her, just stood there staring at him.

"Baby, don't let the water get cold." He pulled her shirt over her head and peeled her jeans off her body. Her underwear followed quickly and he assisted her over into the tub. As much as Jake loved looking at her body, he wanted to take care of her.

Emma looked up and invited, "Sure you don't want to join me?"

"Emma girl, first of all, I don't think I'd ever fit in that tub and second, you need to relax. If I stay here with you naked under those bubbles, you're never gonna relax." With that, Jake headed back to the kitchen to take out the last of the garbage.

A few minutes later, he went back into the bathroom, finding Emma sound asleep with her head resting on the back of the tub. He sat next to the tub and watched her for a while. Her dark air was piled on top of her head, with a few tendrils falling around her face. Dark, thick lashes lay upon her ivory cheeks that were slightly blushed from the warm water. He leaned over the tub and gently placed a kiss on her lips. Emma's eyes fluttered open and she slowly smiled.

"Come on darlin', let's get you out." With that he lifted her out of the tub and patted her dry with a big towel.

"Jake, I can ..." Emma started, but Jake immediately shushed her, shaking his head.

"I know, Emma. You can do it yourself. But I want to," he said simply. Emma just nodded and let him continue to care for her. He then carried her into the bedroom and placed her in the middle of the bed before he stripped and joined her.

That night, Emma and Jake made love. Slow and purposeful, worshipping each other's bodies long into the night. Then they drifted into a peaceful sleep, limbs tangled, breath mingled, heart's beating together.

Chapter 9

Emma awoke, needing to go to the bathroom. Slipping unnoticed from under Jake's arm, she padded softly into the bathroom. Finishing up, she flushed and walked to the sink to wash her hands. As she looked into the mirror, a strange light was reflected in the mirror. Confused, she leaned closer before realizing that the glow was a reflection from the bathroom window. Turning around, she walked to the window to see where the light was coming from. An unusual orange glow was radiating from over the tree tops in her back yard. Staring out of the window for a minute, she tried to force her sleep fogged mind to clear enough to figure out what she was seeing. She grabbed her glasses off of the counter to bring the scene into focus.

Oh my god, NO!

"FIRE JAKE, FIRE!" Emma screamed as she ran through the bedroom, flying out of the door heading down the hall. "Call 911," she continued to scream as she was throwing open the front door.

Jake, jarred awake at her first scream bounded up and out of the bed. He threw on his jeans and jammed his feet into his shoes, grabbing his phone as he followed her down the hall. Assuming the fire was in the house, he couldn't understand why the smoke detectors were not alarming.

"Emma!" he yelled as he pounded down the front porch steps, seeing her running across the yard towards the woods. "Emma!" he yelled again, trying to get her attention. Looking up he saw the orange glow in the woods.

"Goddamn it woman, get back here!" he yelled once more, sprinting across the yard. He caught up to her right before she entered the woods. Grabbing her around the waist, he took her down, rolling over so that he took the impact of the fall and she landed on him.

"Where the hell are you going?" he continued to yell as he rolled over pinning her under him.

"Jake, the woods are on fire, we have to go!" she screamed, struggling to get up.

"Dammit, Emma, you scared the shit out of me. I thought the house was on fire!" Standing up, he reached down to pull her up as well, while pulling out his cell phone. He dialed 911, talked to the dispatch and told them where the fire was. He kept one arm firmly around Emma's shoulders holding her in place. Ending the call, he looked down at her, still wiggling to get free.

"Emma," he said. "Emma, look at me," he ordered. Her frantic eyes looked up and focused on his. "Baby, breathe. The house isn't on fire, we are safe, and the fire department is coming. You are out here with no pants, no shoes, no jacket. Let's go back to the house, wait until Rob and Mac get here and see what needs to be done." Emma slowly nodded.

"Babe, you got me?" he asked gently, holding her chin up so that she had to focus on his face.

Emma took a shaky breath and nodded again. "I got you," she replied softly.

They heard the sirens in the background and started walking back towards the house. The fire truck pulled into her driveway, Mac and Rob jumping out first, running up to Jake and Emma.

"We're fine, we're fine," Jake assured them, knowing that was first on his friends' minds. Pointing towards the woods, Jake said, "My guess is that the old hunting hut is burning."

After several more trucks pulled up, the men start gathering equipment they could haul and plotted the closest way to get to the fire. The hut, while a walkable distance from Emma's house was unable to be accessed directly with a vehicle. There was an old tractor path that followed the western edge of her property, leading around towards the back. Having made their decision, the firemen moved out.

"Babe, stay here. I'm going with them," Jake said, leaning in to kiss Emma's forehead.

The men headed off as Laurie pulled up in her yellow Volkswagen. She hopped out, running up to give Emma a hug. "Oh my gosh, I couldn't believe it when Rob called to say there was a fire here!" The two women walked into the house, heading towards the kitchen.

"We can make coffee for the men when they come back," Emma said as she went over to the kitchen cabinets to pull the coffee down. Her cell phone rang, and she saw Tom's number coming up. "Boy, news travels fast around here," she said as she answered the phone.

"Emma, is Jake there?" Tom asked.

Emma explained that Jake had gone with Rob to take the fire trucks to the old hut. "Do you need him?" she asked.

"We got a call that some kids may have been hanging around in the state park, near the back of your property. I just wanted to let Jake know in case they are still around. I'll keep trying to get him on his cell, and I am heading there now. Mike's already heading out that way."

Hanging up the phone, Emma looked over at Laurie. Explaining what Tom said, she exclaimed, "Laurie, what if the kids are still there? What if they were in the old hut?" Pausing only for a second, Emma grabbed her sneakers near the door, some shorts from the laundry room and started out the back door.

Laurie caught up with her. Looking over at her aunt as they ran through the woods, she yelled, "I can't let you go alone!"

Following a direct path through the woods, the two women ran towards the fire. They could see the fire trucks off to the left as they were making their way towards the hut on an old cart path that ran along Emma's property line. They ran into the clearing seeing the small hut engulfed in flames. Emma ran as close as she could, yelling to see if anyone could hear her.

Laurie grabbed the back of her shirt, shouting "Emma, if anyone was in there, it is too late."

Right then the fire trucks pulled into the clearing from the path and the two women looked over as men began hauling equipment out of the trucks. Emma and Laurie stared into the furious faces of Rob and Jake stalking over to them. Mac, quickly looking over to see that the women were all right, began shouting orders to the other fire fighters.

Emma had never seen Jake so angry. The enraged visage in front of her was nowhere near the gentle lover she come to know. As towering as she knew he was, he seemed to grow larger as he came closer. Feeling intimidated, she began to back up.

"Fuck, woman! What the hell are you doing here?" he cursed. Fury and fear poured off of Jake rivaling the blazing hut.

"Jake I had to come. Tom called and said that some kids were sighted out this way in the state park. I just had to make sure no one was here," Emma pleaded for him to understand. By this time, Jake had reached her. He grabbed her by her upper arms, careful not to hurt her, hauling her backwards, farther away from the fire.

"Jake, please," she said quietly. Jake immediately let her go, took a step back and ran his hand through his hair.

"Emma," he said, walking back a few steps. She could feel the anger pouring off of him, but she was not afraid. She stood quietly, knowing that Jake needed to work through his anger, and he needed some space. She took the chance to look over to see Rob yelling at Laurie and Laurie yelling back.

"Emma," Jake said again, bringing her attention back to his face. "Goddamn it, Em. We drove up, and I swear to God my heart stopped beating when

I saw you tearing through the woods toward that fire."

Emma stepped towards Jake, placing her hand gently over his heart. Looking up into his face, she realized that this huge man, used to protecting everyone, cared for her. And she knew at that moment that she loved him.

I love him. I love him.

"Jake, I am so sorry to have scared you. I just heard that there may have been kids here, and I had to check." She slowly rubbed her hand over his chest where his heart was. "I never meant to frighten you."

Reaching up with his hand, Jake grasped her small hand in his much larger one and held it tight. With his other hand placed behind her head, he pulled her in and lowered his face to hers. His lips met hers in a passionate, smoldering kiss filled with longing, fear, and love.

Emma pulled back looking into his handsome face. Putting both hands on either side of his face, she whispered, "I love you Jake."

Jake closed his eyes, leaning his face into her hands. Reaching down to lift her up, he held her close as she wrapped her legs around his waist. "Emma girl, I love you too," Jake said peering deeply into her eyes.

Emma smiled, at the same time her eyes were tearing up. As she blinked, the tears slid down her cheeks.

"Why are you crying, sweetheart?" Jake asked, continuing to hold her close.

"I've been handling things on my own for so long," she replied.

Jake held her close. "No more, baby. No more. You are mine, and I take care of what is mine."

Walking over to them, Mike called out, "You about ready to get to work or do you two need to get a room?" Emma blushed as Jake set her down. Jake told her to head over to where Laurie was standing.

"And Em," Jake said as she started to walk away. "We will be discussing this stunt you pulled tonight." Emma looked over her shoulder and wisely kept quiet. She knew not to "poke the bear". Smiling at Jake, she turned and walked over to Laurie, who did not look happy.

"Did you just get chewed out?" Emma asked Laurie. Laurie turned and glared at Emma.

"Do you want to know what he said?" Laurie asked, then kept right on ranting. "He told me he couldn't believe that we ran over here. He wanted to know what the hell I thought I was going to do – rush into a burning building? Act like a hero when they were on their way here? Take a chance with my own life needlessly?" Laurie tossed her long brown hair over her shoulders, and barely took a breath before plunging on. "Well, I told him I did not need him telling me what to do! I am an adult, and I can make up my mind on what I will do and not do! Then he told me that he couldn't believe I was so stupid. Stupid? Stupid? He called me stupid."

Emma attempted to interrupt, hoping to calm Laurie down, but Laurie was on a roll.

"So I told him that if I was so stupid, then I was obviously not smart enough for him to bother with and then he stomped off like a little boy!"

Emma reached over and wrapped her arm around Laurie's shoulders.

"Oh Emma, I think we just broke up!" Laurie cried. She turned to Emma, hugging her closely, sobbing.

Emma stroked Laurie's back and said soothing words. Emma was reminded of how many times she had done this very thing; when Laurie was a child and Emma was babysitting her; when their parents died, and Emma comforted her; when Laurie's first boyfriend in high school broke up with her; in college, when Laurie felt stress from all the work. She had always been the person that Laurie turned to and Emma was so glad that she had moved to Fairfield.

"Laurie, you and Rob did not just break up. Rob was just scared honey. Even big, tough Jake told me that his heart almost stopped when they came into the clearing, and he saw me running towards the fire."

Laurie's sobs had turned to sniffles. "Yeah, well I bet Jake didn't call you stupid."

"Well," Emma said. "He didn't say stupid, but you can believe that he was furious."

Laurie looked into Emma's face. "Are you two okay?" she asked.

Emma smiled. "Jake told me he loved me."

Laurie gasped, grabbing her aunt in a huge hug. "Oh God, Emma, I am so happy for you!" she exclaimed.

"Laurie, I promise you and Rob will be okay also. Just look."

The two women looked at the charred wood and ashes that used to be the hut, as the men finished putting out the flames and securing the area. Mac and the others were starting to put away the equipment, and Mike was looking over the sight for evidence.

Jake walked over to Rob and began talking to him. Rob appeared to be arguing back with Jake, but Jake kept talking to him. Both men looked over at the women who were standing there with their arms around each other. The men started walking towards them.

Rob approached Laurie. His face was sooty, and he was pulling off his jacket. His t-shirt was sweaty, plastered to his muscular chest, and Laurie could not help but admire this gorgeous man's physique. Laurie looked up into the eyes of this amazing man who she loved, suddenly realizing that their argument was because he loved her. She did not even wait for him to speak; she jumped into his arms kissing his face.

"Oh Rob, I am so sorry!" she cried. Rob clung to her and began to carry her off towards the truck.

Jake walked over to Emma, who was smiling at Rob and Laurie. She looked up at the man she was giving her heart to and her smile lit up her face.

"What did you say to Rob?" she asked. Jake smiled a slow smile, pulling her close.

"I just reminded him that love makes us crazy when we are afraid for the one we love."

Hugging him tight, she smiled as he was once again acknowledging that he loved her. Emma looked over at the area where the little shack was now a pile of rubble and ash. Mike and Mac were still over there raking through the ashes.

"Do you need to stay for a while?" she asked. "I can catch a ride with Rob and Laurie back to my house."

Right on cue, Mike yelled over to Jake, telling him to go ahead and take Emma home. "Not much here," he said. "I'll stay with Mac a bit and you can go ahead and get your beautiful girl home."

Jake nodded at Mike, "Thanks man. I owe you."

Emma and Jake walked over to one of the trucks where Rob and Laurie were kissing. Rob looked over, giving Jake a head nod, which Emma assumed was man talk for "thank you for keeping me from doing something dumb like walking away from this amazing girl"! They all climbed into the truck, and Rob dropped Emma and Jake off at her house. Laurie said she would pick up her car the next day and headed down the road with Rob.

Emma and Jake walked into the house, locking the door behind them. She began walking down the hall, looking over her shoulder. "Coming to bed Jake?" she asked.

He looked at her, raised his eyebrow, and said in a low voice, "Woman, are you forgetting that we need to deal with your irresponsible actions tonight?"

Emma slowly turned around. "Well, instead of a punishment, I thought you would rather enjoy a celebration. After all, we did declare our love tonight," she said softly with a smile.

Jake, totally enraptured with this beautiful woman he was in love with, couldn't help but grin back.

"What kind of celebration did you have in mind?" he asked.

"Catch me and find out!" Emma called out, as she turned and ran down the hall towards the bedroom. With Jake on her heels, Emma squealed as he captured her around the waist, lifted her up and tossed her on the bed.

Jake pulled his t-shirt over his head, and Emma looked up as his arm muscles flexed, wanting those huge arms wrapped around her. Her eyes lowered to his pecs and abs, following the muscular trail down towards his pants. He toed off his shoes and stepped out of his pants. Emma's eye grew large as she realized he was not wearing any boxers.

"Commando?" she asked.

"Well if you recall, when you were running out of here screaming 'fire', I didn't have a lot of time to get dressed."

Emma blushed and raised her eyes from his impressive cock to his eyes. "I am sorry, baby," she said.

"Hey, this is a celebration, remember?" he said.

Emma smiled and looked back down at his gorgeous body. *How did I ever get such a handsome, wonderful man?*

Jake leaned over and pulled her to the side of the bed. He easily slid her shorts down her legs, noticing that she also was not wearing underwear. Cocking his head to one side, he asked, "Commando, baby?"

"Quick exit, remember?" she answered with a smirk.

Jake lowered himself between her legs, his large hands rubbing circles on her thighs. Emma felt the fire of passion begin to burn with each stroke of his talented hands until...his hands stilled. Raising her head up, she could see Jake staring off to the side of the bed.

"Babe, what did I say about this cat? He's staring at me right now."

Moaning, Emma flopped her head back to the bed. "Jake, stop looking at the cat and take care of me. Mister doesn't know what the hell we're doing."

Feeling the bed shift, she raised her head back up just in time to see Jake plop the cat outside of the bedroom door, shutting it firmly. Turning back around, he resumed his position between her legs, stating, "Not sharin' Emma girl. Not even with Mister."

Starting to giggle, Emma's mirth was quickly replaced with desire as Jake's hands landed back on her body.

His fingers continued upwards on their path, finally reaching their destination. He lowered his head and his lips replaced his fingers as he began slowly licking her wet folds. Emma moaned and pushed her hips forward. Jake placed his hand firmly on her stomach holding her in place. He continued his ministrations adding a finger in her wetness. She writhed as she felt the flames grow higher and higher. He reached up his other hand under her shirt, filling his hand with her breast. He tweaked and pulled on her nipple.

"Jake," Emma called out. "I need you now!"

Jake just chuckled. Emma felt herself give over to the blazing feelings of her orgasm as it sent sparks throughout her core. Emma lay still, breasts rising and falling being the only movement she could manage.

Jake rose up, pushing her t-shirt over her head as he went. Standing, he looked down at Emma. She turned her brilliant smile towards him.

How did I ever get such a dynamic, perfect woman?

Crawling over her body, he made his way onto the bed. Laying down beside her, he stroked her gently, kneading her breasts as he kissed her senseless. Jake felt as though he could not get enough of her.

Suddenly Emma pushed on his shoulders, rolling him on his back as she quickly climbed on top. She leaned down, continuing to kiss him. Their tongues plundered each other's mouths as their hands explored. Emma took his massive cock in her hands and placed the tip at the entrance to her pussy. Slowly she lowered herself down on him. Jake moaned and raised his hips upwards to continue the contact. Emma began to rock up and down on his cock, loving the fullness of it filling her up. She began to feel the tension building again and knew she was close to coming. Jake instinctively took over, rocking his hips forcefully into hers. The pressure built and then intensified as Jake reached up and began to pull on her nipples. Emma screamed out as her orgasm rocked her and Jake followed immediately afterwards. He pulsated into her, continuing to push deep inside of her as he felt his release. With her head on his shoulder, their limbs entwined, their bodies flushed and satisfied for a long time.

Jake loved the feeling of flesh against flesh, no condom. He had never felt so close to anyone in his life.

I don't want this to end. I want this woman with me for always.

Jake pulled out, and Emma curled up next to him. Jake looked at the clock. It was almost three in the morning.

"Go to sleep, baby, it's been a long night," he said. Emma murmured something, but sleep had already started to claim her. Jake held her tight, remembering the horrifying feeling of seeing her run toward the burning shack. Kissing the top of her head as she slept he knew he never wanted to be without this woman as he followed her in sleep.

Chapter 10

A couple of days later Emma sat at in her office talking to Suzy. Tears fell from Suzy's pale blue eyes, so Emma leaned over to hand her a tissue. "I thought he loved me," Suzy said through her sobs. Emma listened patiently, as Suzy described her relationship with Brad. Suzy was tall, willowy and with the same dark hair as her brother, Rob. Emma always thought that she and Brad made a very handsome couple.

"He wouldn't even tell me why he was breaking up with me. He just kept saying that he wasn't good enough for me, and he didn't want to drag me down." Suzy continued to sniffle and hiccup softly, and Emma gave her the chance to cry in peace. But Emma's thoughts were far from peaceful.

Why would Brad say that to Suzy? Was he wanting to find an easy way to let her down? Or does he really think he isn't good enough for her? Brad always had such self-confidence, goals, energy, friendliness. Something is going on, and I'm going to find out what it is.

These thoughts continued to swirl through Emma's head. Keeping Suzy in her office until she was calmer, they talked for a while longer. After Suzy left her office, Emma decided she needed to talk to Brad so she called him down to her office. Brad came in, immediately looking nervous. He slumped down in her chair, and she observed him carefully. His hair was unkempt; he had dark circles under his eyes, and continually shifted in his seat.

Emma was silent, giving Brad a chance to speak first. He finally looked up into her eyes but then quickly lowered his eyes back down.

"Brad, you're not in trouble. I just want to talk. You seem... different... from the young man I met last summer working in my yard." Brad gave a little smile, as though remembering those days made him less nervous. The smile quickly left though and Emma could have sworn she saw regret in his eyes.

"I've been talking to Suzy this morning," she said. Brad glanced up at her, a look of embarrassment crossed his face. Emma spoke, not wanting him to misunderstand the reason for their needed conversation.

"No, Brad, I'm not here to try to talk you into getting back with her. That's not my job. My job is to work with all the students individually – I want to see what *you* need and how I can help *you*." Brad sat, wringing his hands in his lap. He opened his mouth several times to speak but could not seem to decide what to say.

"Brad, my concern is not that you broke up with Suzy. My concern is the reason why you told her you broke up. You have always had such self-confidence. Why would you tell her you are not good enough?" Emma paused, letting her words sink in. Brad raised his eyes up to hers and she noticed that they were bloodshot and teary.

"Brad, what is going on? You can talk to me. Right now, it is you, me and the four walls here. I don't tell anyone about what we talk about unless you are planning to harm yourself or you're involved in something illegal."

At that, Brad sat up quickly, stone faced he looked defiantly at her. "All due respect, Ms. Dodd, I don't have anything I need to tell you," he said.

Smoke. Why am I getting a whiff of smoke?

Emma thoughts were now flying furiously around her mind. Not wanting to scare him off, she knew she needed to tread carefully.

"Brad," she said softly. "I just want you to feel as though you can talk to me. You're smart, good-looking, great personality, athletic. You have so much going for you, but your behaviors are changing right before my eyes. I care about you."

Brad's defiance slipped away, and once again she saw a small boy in front of her, struggling with some secret.

"Ms. Dodd, you're right. I haven't been myself, but I promise I'm taking care of it. I've just been under a lot of stress lately." Emma sat quietly, letting the silence bring peace between them. As a counselor, she knew the value of silence – it can allow someone to organize their thoughts until they will continue to speak.

Sure enough, Brad began to speak, confessing, "I feel bad about Suzy, but I just have so much going on. I gotta get my grades up, keep up with sports, my part time job, and just stuff that is weighing me down." Looking down, he took a deep breath. "I'm getting it together, Ms. Dodd. I promise."

Raising his head, he stared directly into her eyes, and Emma felt that whatever he was dealing with and hiding, he was truthful about wanting to work it out. But she still felt some fear for him. If he had been near the fire last night then he was definitely out in the park area and probably doing something he shouldn't be doing.

"All right, Brad. You can head back to class now. Just know that I care, and you can talk to me anytime." Emma wrote a pass for him, and they stood up. Brad started to leave then turned suddenly and gave her a big hug.

"Thank you, Ms. Dodd. I…. well, just thank you." Emma hugged back, wanting to smile at the show of confidence, but she couldn't help but notice….. Brad's jacket definitely smelled of smoke. Not cigarette smoke. No, this was the distinct smell of smoke from a wood fire.

Debating who to talk to first, Emma decided to go back to the coach with her concerns. Coach Ted was definitely the best choice, if she wanted someone who could influence Brad. Heading to the gym after school, she remembered her earlier trip there in the fall. She found Ted as he came out of the locker room.

"Litl'bit – what's up?" he said in his familiar greeting. "Need to talk again over dinner?" he joked.

Emma laughed. "I think we'll just talk here if you don't mind – I'd hate for people to get the wrong idea," she joked back.

They walked into the gym, sitting down on the bleachers. Not wanting to break Brad's confidentiality, Emma was careful in divulging too many details. She told Ted her concerns over the breakup, which was common knowledge, and the reasons he gave. She also admitted her concerns about his change in appearance, grades, and anxiety. Knowing that Ted cares a great deal about "his boys" as he likes to call them, she was surprised that he seemed agitated.

"Emma, I just think you are making more of it than there is. He hasn't done anything wrong. Yeah, his grades are slipping some, but it's probably just senioritis. He's a hard worker, doesn't miss practice, and I really don't want you hounding him."

"Ted, I'm not hounding him. I just want to see if I can help in some way. I thought you could help as well," Emma replied.

"It seems that you're more upset with him breaking up with his girlfriend and making a mountain out of a molehill," Ted continued. "You need to realize that my boys don't need to be babied. He'll be fine. He'll graduate, go on to college with a football or wrestling scholarship, and it won't hurt lil' Suzy to move on."

Incensed, Emma was confused at Ted's attitude. *What is going on? Is Ted knowingly ignoring a problem with one of "his boys"?*

As much as she hated to give in, Emma knew that Ted was not only not going to help, he definitely wanted her to back off. Plastering on a fake smile, she looked up at Ted. "Coach, I'm sure you're right. Thanks for letting me know I have nothing to worry about," she said sweetly.

Standing up from the bleachers, Ted gave her a big grin. "That's a girl," he said encouragingly. "My boys'll be fine."

Emma walked back to her office, grabbed her purse, and decided to pay Jake a visit at the police station. Something was up, and she had a suspicious feeling that Ted may be in on it. Walking into the station, she greeted Sally, the police receptionist.

"Hey Emma, here to see Jake?" the older woman called. Emma looked over at the woman who kept track of everything going on with the Fairfield Police Station. She couldn't help but grin – Sally had been in place since before computers and Emma was sure that Sally was just as knowledgeable as a computer anyway.

"Yes. Is he here?" Emma asked.

"Sorry dear, he's out with Tom right now. I don't know when he will be back," Sally replied.

Just then, Mike walked through the main doors behind Emma. "Emma" he greeted. "What brings you here? Well, besides checking up on one of our finest?" he joked.

"I had something that I was suspicious of and wanted to talk to Jake, but I guess it will have to wait."

Mike's professionalism kicked in immediately as he went into detective mode. "Well, Emma, we work on most of the same cases. Perhaps I can help or at least hear you out." Emma thought for a second, then realized that she really wanted to get her suspicions out in case it was time sensitive.

"Sure, that would be great," she answered.

Mike led Emma down the hall to an office, offered her a seat and pulled out a pad of paper.

"Have you found any evidence from my fire last night?" Emma started.

Mike looked up. "Well, it's an open investigation, so I can't officially report on it, but you were there so you saw that the hut was completely burned. I will tell you that the fire marshal hasn't given a report yet, but I didn't see anything unusual from the wreckage. Why do you ask?"

Emma thought carefully how to answer. "Tom called last night to tell Jake that a park ranger had seen some kids on the back of the property near the hut earlier. Then today, one of my students smelled like smoke."

Mike's sharp eyes glanced from the pad of paper back up to her face. "Is that it? Just that they smelled like smoke?"

"Well, no. This student has been changing. Grades are poor, appearance unkempt, broke up with his girlfriend, looks like he hasn't slept. And then today, he smelled like smoke."

Mike jotted down notes, then looked back up at her. "You gonna tell me who the student is?"

Emma hesitated. "Mike, I don't want to make things worse for this student. I'm just concerned."

"Look Emma. What you are doing is helping in an active investigation. I'm not going to run out and arrest anyone." Emma smiled at that. Mike continued, "What I will do is take the information you give me, do some checking on my own without sharing with anyone else at this time. If it appears it has nothing to do with this investigation, I'll keep it between you and me. If I find that there is some evidence of being part of this investigation, I will share that with the other detectives and we will act on it. Emma, that is the same thing that Jake would be doing if he were here right now."

At that, Emma nodded in understanding. "Okay," she answered. "So right now, this just stays between us until you have a chance to check it out. And if nothing comes from that, you won't let everyone know the student's name."

"I promise," Mike answered.

Emma took a deep breath. "The student I am concerned about is Brad Evans, Wendy and Bill's son," she confessed.

"The football player?" Mike asked incredulously. "I can't see him wanting to risk a college scholarship doing something stupid like setting a hut on fire."

"I know it seems crazy, but I see so many changes in him, and he smelled like smoke this morning," she reiterated. "But there is more." At this she hesitated. "But Mike before I continue, I have to know that this information isn't going to get out everywhere. I do not want to be responsible for the police possibly ruining innocent lives."

Mike nodded. "Emma, I have promised – what you tell me today stays between us. I will check things out quietly just to see if there is any basis in your concerns."

Again, Emma took a deep breath. "Okay. I also took my concerns to Coach Ted. He not only dismissed them, he told me that I needed to forget them and drop the whole thing." Mike nodded slowly this time, keeping his eyes on her. "I mean, why wouldn't he be concerned about one of 'his boys' as he likes to call them? He actually seem to be chastising me for caring!"

Mike jotted a few more notes down, then reached over and patted her hands. "Look Emma, I can tell this whole thing is upsetting you. Have you talked to anyone else about your concerns?"

"No," she replied. "No one."

"Here's what I am going to do. I'm not going to mention this to anyone – not even Jake or Tom at the moment. Let me do a little checking up on things myself, just to see if I can find any evidence linking Ted or Brad to your fire. If not, we will let this drop. But Emma, if I do find some link, your testimony will be needed in this case." Mike looked at her sharply to see if she understood.

Emma nodded in agreement. "I understand. And Mike – thank you so much. I feel so much better knowing someone else can check into them for me!"

They stood up from the table, and Mike escorted her outside.

At that moment Jake was coming up the station's front stairs. His eyes narrowed as he saw Mike's hand on Emma's back.

Emma turned around, saw Jake and her smile lit up her face. "Jake, I came looking for you!"

Reaching down, Jake drew Emma into his embrace, and away from Mike.

Mike laughed at his friend's response. "Don't worry pal. She sure as hell didn't smile like that for me."

Jake looked over at Mike, gave him a head jerk and pulled Emma around to his side. "You okay, babe?" he asked Emma kissing her on the top of her head.

"Yeah, just a rough day at work," she replied, hugging him close. "I thought I would stop in and see you. Mike kept me company though since you weren't available," she joked.

Jake scowled and swatted her ass, noting the tight pencil skirt cupping that gorgeous bottom. *Damn, I never had a teacher that looked like her when I was in high school.* Suddenly, Jake found himself jealous of the teens that got to view her beauty every day.

Emma squealed and hopped into her car. Rolling the car window down, she smiled just for him, as Jake leaned onto her car.

"I was going to call you in a bit," Jake said. "Mom wanted to know if you would like to come to dinner."

Emma's smile grew wider. "I would love to. You know I love your mom. What time?"

"I can pick you up about six o'clock," Jake answered.

Emma looked confused. "Honey, you don't have to pick me up. I can just come over."

"I don't want you going back into your house by yourself that late at night. I'll come pick you up," Jake said definitively.

Emma just smiled and nodded. Jake was protective and there was no arguing with him when he was in that mode. *He will be great with children.* Emma knew it was early to be thinking about children, but for her, Jake was it. Everything she wanted. Everything she needed. Continuing to smile, she drove away, waving to Jake and Mike standing on the steps of the police station.

Chapter 11

"Mrs. Campbell, dinner was delicious," Emma said, as she rose to start clearing the table. Emma enjoyed having dinner with Jake and his mother. It reminded her of dinners when she was much younger and the family would sit around the table, talking about their day. Emma often found that it was the simple things that made her think of home and miss her family.

"My dear, I have told you to call me, Mary," Jake's mom said. Emma smiled at her, as Jake leaned down and kissed his mother's cheek.

"We'll take care of the cleanup since you cooked," he said. "You head on into the living room, and I'll have Emma get the coffee."

Mary nodded appreciatively and prepared to rise from the table. Emma noticed how Jake discreetly assisted his mother to a standing position, making sure she was steady before moving away. After making quick work of the cleaning, they settled in with their coffees in the living room. Mary was seated in a comfortable chair that Emma noticed had sturdy arms on it that could be used to help Mary sit or rise by herself. She also noticed that the warm, inviting house had no clutter.

Emma walked around admiring the pictures on the walls. Mary also decorated her house in family pictures. Emma viewed pictures showing a much younger Jake, along with his mother and father. She stared at the picture of Jake as a small boy, tousled blond hair blowing in the wind, as he held up a fishing pole complete with a dangling fish on the end. Jake looked to be a carbon copy of his father, a large man with a ready smile and bright blue eyes. In one photo, Jake's father was looking at his wife and Emma could see the love that poured off of that giant of a man.

I want that. I want a picture of Jake looking at me just the way his father is looking at his mother.

Emma also saw a few pictures of three little boys, at the same fishing hole, holding up a string of fish between them. Upon closer inspection, she realized that she was looking at Jake, Rob, and Tom – all about the age of ten.

"Oh my goodness, is this who I think it is?" she exclaimed. "You guys were so cute back then!"

Mary laughed and Jake wondered aloud, "Don't you think we're still cute?"

Emma turned from perusing the pictures and walked over to him. As she walked closer she had to keep tilting her head back farther to see into his smiling eyes. She rose up on her tiptoes and Jake obliged by leaning down a little. She gave him the softest kiss and placed her hand on his chest over his heart.

"I'm not sure cute is the word I would use to describe you, Mr. Campbell," she whispered with a saucy grin.

"And just what word would you use, Ms. Dodd?" Jake asked with one eyebrow raised in question, clasping tightly to her hand pressed between them.

"Hmmm, perhaps that is a question best answered when we are alone." Emma couldn't repress her smile at the look of pure lust that flashed across Jake's face. Squeezing his hand, she turned and walked over to the sofa.

The three of them continued to chat amiably for a while, Mary regaling Emma with stories of Jake's childhood adventures and misadventures. Emma laughed until her sides hurt and Jake actually blushed at a few of his mom's tales.

"Well my dears, it's getting late and I think I'll head to bed now. Thank you so much for coming, Emma. It was delightful, and I want to see a lot more of you," she said with a wink. As she hugged

Emma goodbye, she whispered in her ear. Smiling, Emma nodded as she embraced Mary. Jake raised his eyebrow in silent question, but Emma shook her head and stepped back.

Grinning, he leaned over to kiss the top of her head. "I'll be right back, babe. I just want to make sure mom is settled for the night." Emma nodded and took the coffee cups into the kitchen to wash them out. A few minutes later, Jake came back into the kitchen wrapping his arms around her from behind.

Emma leaned back and felt his arms tighten. "Ummmm, I love you wrapped around me."

"Emma girl, when we get back to your house, you're gonna feel all of me wrapped around you."

Emma turned in his arms and locked her arms around his neck. "Promise?" she asked.

"Guarantee," he said, leaning down to kiss her. The kiss deepened and as Emma moaned appreciatively, Jake took the opportunity to slip his tongue into her mouth. She tasted of chocolate and coffee he thought delightfully. Tongues tangoed in an erotic dance. Slipping one hand down to cup Emma's ass, he kneaded it before lifting her up on the counter. Continuing the kiss, he grasped her face, angling it so that he could deepen the kiss even more. Emma began to moan, rubbing her pussy on his jeans. Feeling his erection pressing against her, all she could think was how much she wanted him in her.

Jake slid his hands from her face down to her breasts. He unbuttoned the top several buttons to allow her blouse to be pushed off of her shoulders. Exposing her black lacy bra, he looked down at her luscious breasts spilling out of the top of her bra. Sliding his lips down, he nuzzled the bra cups down and grasped her nipple in his mouth. Laving and tugging on her nipple, Jake continued his ministrations on the other breast. Emma felt a jolt of electricity straight from her nipple to her core. She continued to squirm and wiggle, trying to get her aching pussy closer to the bulge in Jake's jeans. Jake kissed his way back up from her breast to her mouth, exploring her mouth thoroughly. Slowly he pulled himself away and Emma moaned in agony. She felt the cool air hit her exposed breasts and her swollen lips tingled with the loss of contact. He leaned over and gently pulled her bra cups back into place and slid her blouse back over her shoulders. Emma slowly looked up into his baby blue eyes and noticed the twinkle.

"Babe, we need to get you home. If we stay here, I am going to fuck you on my mom's dining room table. While that thought has me hard, I don't think you want my mom possibly walking in."

Emma took a deep breath trying to still her erratic heartbeat, then smiled slowly up at him. "I love you, Jake Campbell," she said as he assisted her off the counter.

Pulling her in for a tight hug, Jake kissed the top of her head. "Come on, darlin', let me get you home."

Emma nodded in agreement, slipping her small hand into his much larger one as they made their way out to his truck.

Once at her house, Jake took the keys from her so that he could enter first. Huffing, Emma complained that she was perfectly capable of going into her house by herself. Jake asked her wait by the front door as he made a sweep of the rooms. Understanding that his request was important to him, she waited, although not so patiently. Seeing her tap her foot as he walked back over, he wrapped his arms around her tiny frame, pulling her close.

"Baby, I know you are capable, but I'm gonna protect you every chance I get with everything I have."

Leaning her head back to look into his piercing stare, she couldn't help but smile. Feeling protected, feeling cherished, feeling loved.

"Take me to bed," she said softly. "Make love to me."

"Oh, Emma girl, it would be my pleasure," Jake answered back reverently. He carried her to the bedroom, setting her down next to the bed. Slowly peeling her clothes off, he felt as though he was unwrapping a present. As he exposed her breasts, his hands palmed each one, measuring its fullness. Her nipples hardened and ached for his touch. Instinctively knowing what she needed, he rolled them between his forefinger and thumb, pinching slightly.

Emma reached up, pulling on his shirt until he could shrug it off. Jake and Emma continued to undress each other until they stood bare, no clothes, no fears, no inhibitions.

Turning slowly, Emma walked the few step to the bed, where she lay down on her back, raising her arms up towards Jake.

He stood for a moment, looking down at this beautiful woman who wanted him. Lying there, waiting for him to love her. Not willing to waste another second, Jake moved to the bed and her awaiting arms. Holding her close, feeling her heartbeat against his chest, he kissed her with the reverence of a man in love.

Emma felt the change in Jake. The air in the room was not only charged with sexual tension, but with an overpowering sensation of affection. This time, he truly was making love. Their kisses intensified as they explored each other's mouths. Their hips began the age old mating dance of pressing on each other, as she grew wet and he felt the pleasure of his dick moving against her. Emma felt as though she would explode, but from what, she wasn't sure. The emotion of the moment was consuming.

Sliding his fingers into her wetness, Jake moved them in just the right rhythm to have her finally peak, splintering into a thousand pieces. Jake continually kissed her, positioning himself at her entrance. Seating himself with one plunge, he felt connected to her in every way. *Heart, soul, body, life.*

Slow, languid strokes of his cock into her accepting body, Emma desired to hold on to these feelings forever.

Jake's strokes increased in pace, but not in harshness. Continuing to worship her body, he felt his release coming. She raised her legs to allow him deeper access and a few strokes later she felt her second orgasm explode. Jake pulsated inside, feeling the delicious sensation of spilling inside.

After a few minutes of blissful unawareness, Jake raised up on his arms, looking down on the woman, who captured his heart. Her face flushed with passion, he had never seen a more beautiful woman. Eyes bright, china doll complexion, and long silky hair sweeping the pillow.

Emma looked up at his baby blues, feeling as though she could drown in them. She didn't want to move. She didn't want him to pull out. She didn't want him to leave her body, leave her bed, leave her house. Smiling, she pulled him down, placing her lips on his, putting all of her emotions into a slow, languid kiss.

Driving back home early the next morning, Jake thought about Emma.

I know what I want...Emma as my wife. I want to make love to her every night and wake up to her beautiful face every morning. But what about mom?

Jake knew that Emma loved his mother and Mary certainly loved Emma, but how to have them both together? Emma loved her new house and he would love living there with her, but his mom's disability would worsen and he needed to be available to assist her.

Shaking his head as though to clear it, he arrived home with no easy solution in mind.

Chapter 12

Tom, Jake, and Mike were at their desks when Tom's cell phone rang. Looking down at it, he saw it was Carol.

"Hey gorgeous," he answered. "What's up?" Suddenly Tom sat up straight, grabbed a pen, and started scribbling. "Are they still alive?" he asked. Jake and Mike looked at each other, on alert. "Be there soon, Carol."

Turning to the others, he quickly gave them the information. "Carol said that two kids from the high school have been brought in. Both high on something, one acting aggressive. She said their parents have been called and the school's resource officer is at the hospital." Looking directly at Jake, he continued. "Emma's there too."

"This may be the break we need," Jake said as he was already heading out the door. Tom and Mike were right on his heels. Jumping into Jake's truck, they headed to the hospital.

Striding into the ER, the three detectives flashed their badges at the guard's desk and were told to head back to Bays 5 and 6. As they were walking down the hall, they were met with a patrol officer. As he was giving them the details, Jake looked up, seeing Emma outside one of the rooms talking to a couple that he assumed were the parents. Jake looked at Tom and jerked his head towards Emma. Tom nodded in understanding and kept going over the information with the patrolman. Jake walked toward Emma, but stayed a discreet distance while she comforted the parents.

Her arms were around the woman sobbing on Emma's shoulders. Next to her, Emma looked so petite, but Jake realized what strength that tiny frame contained. Emma held the crying woman, continuing to talk to the father.

"Mr. Jacobs, they are doing everything they can. We got to them quickly and got them here."

She continued to rub the Mrs. Jacob's back, while trying to calm her husband. The doctor came out to speak to the Jacobs.

Jake noticed Emma was trying to discreetly step back to give them privacy, but Mrs. Jacobs would not let go of her. *She is everything. She cares with her whole heart. She gives without ever thinking of taking back. She loves with her whole being. I'm one lucky SOB to have her and I'm gonna find a way to keep her and never let her go.*

The Jacobs followed the doctor into their child's room while Emma stood.

"Emma," Jake spoke softly.

Recognizing his voice, Emma turned and ran the few steps into Jake's waiting arms. Holding him tight, she listened as his heartbeat filled her with a sense of calm and rightness.

Jake knew she would speak when she felt as though she could. He kept his embrace firmly around her, willing her to feel his comfort. Tom and Mike walked up and stood behind them. Carol, sliding next to her husband found herself wrapped protectively his arms. Tom and Mike had already spoken to the patrolman, but allowed Emma to tell them what information the doctor had given.

"The boys will be fine according to the doctor. They were smoking pot before school this morning, which is not unusual for these boys. But it appears that is may have been laced with something, possibly heroin. They were speaking sluggishly, appeared intoxicated, and one of them became belligerent when a teacher approached them. The police were called when the nurse suspected drug use, and the principal asked me to come as the school representative." After reciting the factual information, Emma suddenly felt very tired, the exhaustion draining every ounce of energy.

Wrapping his arm tighter around her, Jake allowed her to lean her slight weight against him. He looked down at her pale face. "Babe, let me take you home," he said gently.

Emma nodded her acquiescence. "Since the parents are here, I am relieved of my school duty," she explained, "so I can leave whenever you are ready."

Carol walked over to her friend, hugging her. "Jake, you finish up here, and I'll take Emma to the cafeteria." Thanking Carol, he watched the two women walk down the hall, arms around each other in support.

Mike watched the women as well, then turned to Tom and Jake. "You guys have two of the nicest, not to mention prettiest women in this whole town. Damn bastards," he jokingly grumbled. Jake and Tom agreed as they all turned back to continue the investigation.

Carol's shift was over before Jake was finished with his questioning. She volunteered to take Emma back to her car, which was left at the school. Emma hugged the petite blonde, noticing how very thin she was. She hoped she was not ill, but knew that Carol hated to talk about her weight. Driving home, she was lost in thoughts of everything that had happened that day.

I hate that weed is so easy for the kids to get hold of, but now if it is laced with harder drugs that just makes it worse. Her thoughts turned to the kids whose grades were slipping or behavior was changing. *What about Brad? Is he involved in drugs? As an athlete, would he chance his scholarship?*

Her mind continued to think of all of the strange events over the past couple of months, but like a puzzle that was missing some pieces, she just could not see a pattern.

How are they getting weed with heroin? How many kids are involved? Do they even know their weed is laced? Who is getting these drugs to the kids? Why did Ted not want me involved? No way, she chastised herself. *There is no way the coach would be involved. And yet he was so adamant that she leave "his boys" alone.*

Emma arrived at home, no wiser for all of her musings. She parked in the driveway and headed up her porch steps. It was dark; she had anticipated being home earlier and had not left the porch light on.

Feeling her way up the dark porch steps, she stubbed her toe on something next to the front door as she was trying to get her keys. She couldn't see what it was, but assumed the postman must have left a package. Opening the front door, she leaned in and turned on the porch light, as Mister shot out of the door. Turning back around, she looked down in horror.

A dead animal, its carcass ripped open, spilled out on the porch mat. She jerked back and started to grab her cell phone to call Jake. Before slamming the front door, she noticed a slip of paper lying on the mat. Looking around, the front yard was quiet, and she saw nothing else unusual. Slowly bending down, as if in a trance, Emma picked up the piece of paper and then carefully backed into the house, slamming the door. Remembering her cat was still outside, she opened the door, grabbing Mister as he sniffed the carcass. Slamming the door again, she set the alarm for the house before moving into the living room to look at the note. It was written on simple white computer paper.

**stop interfering and no one will get hurt –
if you tell your police boyfriend the first
one hurt will be a student and you know
who I mean**

Emma sat down on the sofa, holding the note in her shaking fingers. She kept staring at the words as though if she read them over and over again, she would understand them. Her heart was pounding and the desire to call Jake was overwhelming.

Don't be hasty. Don't call him yet. Someone may be watching.

She jumped up and quickly closed all of the curtains and blinds. Walking into the kitchen, she turned on the coffee maker.

This is going to be a long night. I just need to think it through, figure it out.

Emma knew that Jake would be furious if he found out that she had been threatened, but she couldn't take the chance that someone would get hurt by telling him. Taking her coffee back into the living room, she sat back down on the sofa holding the note in her hands again. Mister curled up next to her as though to assist with the task.

Think Emma, you need to figure out what is going on.

stop interfering

Emma thought back to everything she had done with her students, that could possibly be considered interfering. She had looked into students who seem to be changing. She had talked to several of them, thinking of Brad in particular. She dismissed Brad; she knew he would never have left the dead animal or the note. She also did not think that students would leave a note that referred to someone else as a **student.** No, the threat had to be coming from an adult. The only adult she had spoken to about the boys was Ted.

Ted? Could it possibly be Ted? No. No?

Emma's thoughts raced through her mind, desperately trying to reconcile the Coach Ted that loves "his boys" and the man who seemed almost angry that she was wanting to talk to them.

police boyfriend

Emma realized that that could be anyone since it was well known in town now that she and Jake were dating. *I'm not getting anywhere!*

you know who I mean

Emma thought of all the students she dealt with.

Why does this person think I know who they will hurt? I don't even know who is involved.

Emma remembered her conversation with Brad that led to her talking with Coach Ted.

Smoke. I smelled smoke on Brad. Somehow, someway he is involved.

She looked at the clock and realized that it was late. Knowing she wasn't going to make any more headway tonight, she took the note, folded it back up and tucked it between some books on her bookshelf. Heading to bed, she hoped that she would be able to sleep.

Early the next morning, Emma went out on the front porch knowing she needed to take care of the carcass that had been left the night before, and she wanted to do it before Jake came around. She took her dust pan with some plastic bags and scooped it up. Trying not to gag, she carried the carcass to the edge of the woods and disposed of it. Getting back to her front porch, she made sure to clean up the area, tossing the mat into the garbage can. She quickly got ready for work and headed out.

Pulling into the teacher's parking lot, she found herself looking around as she got out of the car. The hair on her neck began to prickle, and she could feel someone's eyes on the back of her. Emma turned slowly, looking behind her, seeing Ted standing next to his truck. He stared at her, holding her gaze for a moment before giving a little head tilt and walking away.

That was creepy! Or am I just being paranoid?

Shaking her head to clear her thoughts, she walked toward the school. Once inside, she noticed Brad leaning against some lockers staring at her also. Normally Brad would give her a friendly greeting, but today he startled when he saw her looking at him, then quickly turned and walked away.

The day was finally over, and Emma was exhausted. Little sleep the night before, combined with racing thoughts all during the day, had Emma longing for a glass of wine and bed. Her phone chirped, and looking down she saw Laurie's name. Grinning, she answered quickly.

"Hey girl, what's up?"

"I haven't seen you in the past few days and I miss my auntie Em," Laurie joked. "Plus Carol and I want to have a girl's night out. Please come with us," Laurie begged.

"God, I would love to!" Emma said. "I'm so beat, but I really need some serious girl time!"

"Everything okay?" Laurie asked, not remembering hearing Emma sound quite so desperate before.

"Yeah. Just stress. Job, fire, life," Emma tried to joke. "Where are we meeting?"

"Where else? Smokey's," Laurie declared. "About six o'clock all right with you? We were going to have dinner there as well. Tom and Jake are still at work, and Rob is on shift tonight."

"Sounds perfect. See you then," Emma replied, secretly glad she would not have to see Jake tonight, knowing how hard it would be to keep the threat against her a secret.

As Emma approached her car she noticed Ted standing near it. She looked straight into his eyes, determined not to show any fear or give away any anger.

"Ted. What can I do for you?" she said in a steady voice.

"Emma," he replied. "I was just wondering if you'd thought anymore about what we talked about the other day. About not hassling my boys."

Shocked, Emma stated emphatically, "Ted, I will do whatever I have to do to protect these students."

Misunderstanding her meaning, her answered seem to satisfy him. "Good, good. I just don't want anything to happen to keep my boys from scholarships." He smiled and nodded at her as he began to walk away. "You take care now, you hear?" he said over his shoulder.

Oh my God, Emma thought. *The audacity. Is he the one who is threatening me?*

Jumping in her car, she slammed the door, and headed home. Pulling up to her house, she saw Jake sitting on her porch swing. *Damn.* Normally, she would be thrilled to see him, but emotions were churning and she wasn't sure she could keep them hidden.

As she got out of the car, he jogged down the steps and over to her. Picking her up, he gave her a big hug as he swung her around. "God, I've missed you babe," he said burying his head in her hair. He and Tom had spent most of the day chasing leads that led to nowhere. Tired and frustrated, he wanted to see her before heading back out.

"I've missed you too Jake."

He set her down, piercing her with his gaze, not liking what he saw. "Emma girl, what's wrong?" Jake questioned.

Emma sighed. It was both wonderful and a curse that Jake could read her so easily.

"Nothing." She looked up at him, noticing that her answer had elicited a raised eyebrow. She couldn't help but giggle at his look. He didn't even need to speak to make her know that he expected an answer and it had better be an honest one. Emma sighed as he set her down, keeping his massive arms wound tightly around her.

Safe. Secure. Wanted. Cherished.

Emma realized she felt all of those things as she rested in the security of Jake's embrace. Looking back up, she determined to be honest without giving away too much. "Jake, I did not sleep well last night and then today was just a really bad day at work."

Jake held her eyes, until he was satisfied with her answer, but not liking the feeling of helplessness he felt.

Wanting to change the subject as quickly as possible, she told him about her dinner plans. "Laurie said that you and Tom would be working late, so we girls are going to have dinner at Smokey's. Carol is coming too."

Jake hated that Emma would be at a bar without him, but knew how responsible she was. Plus he trusted Laurie and Carol. *But fuck, three gorgeous women at a bar by themselves!*

"Babe, I hate not seeing you tonight," he confessed.

"I know. I miss not sleeping beside you," she said. Pressing her body as close to him as she could, she purred, "and I really hate not having this hot body naked beside me!"

Jake groaned as he felt his cock strain against his pants and pressed his erection tightly against her pelvis. He leaned down and took her mouth in a possessive kiss. His tongue plunged inside, swirling around her mouth, tangling with her tongue. The kiss deepened. Emma found herself on the receiving end of a kiss that made her nipples peak and her pussy clench. She moaned and continued to try to press her swollen clit against his erection. She desperately wanted to relieve the pressure that was growing. Jake picked her up, never breaking the kiss, briskly walking towards the front door. Once inside, he turned and pressed her against the door. Emma giggled against his mouth.

"I think we've been here before, sailor," she joked.

"Gotta get back to work babe. Can you take this quick and hard?"

Emma, turned on by his words as much as if he had spouted poetry, grabbed his head in her hands and plundered his mouth in a toe curling kiss. Jake pushed her shirt up with one hand and quickly pulled down the cups of her bra. Her breasts came free right at the level of his mouth. He sucked one nipple into his mouth deeply and Emma felt the familiar tug in her core. She continued to try to rub her aching clit against his bulge.

"Hold on darlin'. You're going to make this end before I get started," Jake admonished.

"Jake, I can't wait. Please fuck me!" Emma pleaded.

Growling, he pushed her skirt up over her hips and grasping her panties with his free hand he ripped them, tossing them to the floor. Using that same hand, he unzipped his pants, pushing them down to free his aching cock. Emma circled her legs higher on his hips to make herself more accessible. Jake pushed his fingers deep inside.

"Soaked, babe. You're soaked for me." Pulling his hand out, he reached for his cock and centered it at her pussy. "Ready, Em?" he asked, desperately hoping the answer would be *yes!*

"Jaaaake," Emma moaned, "Now!"

Jake pushed up hard into her wet pussy all the way to his balls. Emma slammed her head against the door as she moaned at the fullness she felt. Her fingernails raked against his shoulders as she held on tightly. Jake continued to slam into her over and over until Emma screamed his name as she found her release and pulsated tightly around his cock. Jake plundered her mouth again, kissing her until she wasn't sure where she ended and he began. Jake felt his balls tighten, and then he surged deep inside of her. They stayed pressed against the door, panting heavily, letting the euphoria surround them. Slowly, floating back down to earth, Jake gently pulled out and lowered her to the floor.

Looking deeply into her eyes, he held her close. "Are you all right, Emma girl?" he asked, pushing her hair back from her face. Emma looked up into the bluest eyes she had ever seen and smiled.

"I'm perfect," she purred. "We're perfect. Just being with you, makes my world so much better."

Jake brought his hands up to cup her face. He peered into her dark chocolate eyes. "I love you Ms. Dodd," he said with a smile.

"I love you back, Mr. Campbell," she answered with a grin.

Jake could not believe his good fortune. Five months ago, he had been alone, working long hours and taking care of his mother. He did not begrudge any of those things, certainly not taking care of his mother, and he really enjoyed his job. But the being alone…. well that was something he had convinced himself did not bother him. Once Tom and Carol got married and then Rob found Laurie, he found that he felt more than just being alone – he felt lonely.

Then Emma walked into his life, and nothing was the same. *Tell her. Don't be an ass – tell her what she means to you.*

"Emma," Jake said seriously. At the tone of his voice, Emma looked up questioningly. "I don't know what I did to deserve you, but I plan on spending the rest of my life living to earn your devotion. I've been alone for a long time, and you make me not want to be alone anymore," he said softly, holding her close with their hands clasped between them.

Emma could feel tears forming in her eyes at his words. It had been years since she had felt so cherished.

Jake continued, "I know you have been on your own since you were eighteen. You raised and took care of Laurie, changing your whole world to give her the life you knew she deserved."

Emma opened her mouth to speak, but Jake put his fingers over her kiss swollen lips.

"No, let me finish," he said. Emma nodded, understanding this was important to him. "I know you say you didn't give up anything raising her so I won't argue the point. But you *did* change your life and changed it greatly. You do that so naturally. You put others first. You do it in your job. You do it with your friends. And I have felt you do it with me. But Emma darlin', remember what I said a long time ago when you were swimming in that pool?"

Emma grinned at the memory and nodded. "You said I had better get used to you taking care of me," she answered softly.

"You make me a better man and one who plans on taking care of you from now on."

Staring at the gorgeous man standing in front of her, declaring his feelings. Emma could not believe her good fortune. He was everything she could have ever wanted.

You are keeping something from him.

She pushed those thoughts from her head, knowing she had no choice if she were going to keep everyone safe. Smiling back up at him, she touched her hand to his chest, over his heart.

"I love you, Jake," she declared.

Emma's cuckoo clock on the wall chimed and they both startled. "Oh my god, I'm going to be late!" she exclaimed.

"Yeah, Tom is gonna wonder where I have been," Jake complained. He helped straighten her clothing, and with a quick kiss and a warning to be safe, he headed back out of the door. He hated that she was going to be at a bar without him tonight, but was satisfied that enough people in town now knew that they were dating. Plus Bill and Wendy would be handling the bar so the girls would be well protected. Jake trusted Bill, knowing he would not hesitate to call him or Tom if there were any problems.

Emma quickly showered and changed into a casual outfit. After wearing heels all day, she was glad for the excuse to throw on some dark skinny jeans and a navy long sleeve blouse. Pairing that with her comfortable boots she was ready to head out of the front door. She was excited to spend some time with girlfriends, never having time to do that when she was younger. Careful to turn on all of the outside lights, she also left lights on inside as well. She double checked to see that the security system was alarmed and the doors locked.

I guess it was a good idea that Jake insisted on an alarm system. Grinning to herself, Emma hopped into her car and headed out.

Chapter 13

Emma walked in, seeing Laurie and Carol sitting at the bar talking to Wendy. Laurie always complained that she had to wear comfortable shoes during the workday as an elementary school teacher, so Emma wasn't surprised to see her in her four inch heeled boots. Carol, as always, looked impeccable in her designer jeans.

"Hey girls!" she called out in greeting. The three women looked over and smiled back.

"Hey Bill," she said as she hopped up on a bar stool, leaning over to hug her friends. Bill looked over and scowled at the three women sitting at the bar.

"What's wrong with Bill?" she asked Wendy. Wendy just looked over at her husband and laughed. Laurie and Carol burst into laughter as well. "What am I missing?" Emma asked.

"Tom called earlier and told Bill that he was supposed to look after us tonight to make sure no other men were hanging around," Carol answered, tossing her blonde hair back away from her face, showing off her delicate features.

Laurie, never at a loss for words, jumped in. "Rob called also, not knowing that Tom had called, and told Bill that he was holding him personally responsible for us," she said through giggles.

Wendy finished up the tale, as she continued to wipe down the bar in front of them. "Then guess who called next?" Emma looked up at the beautiful older woman.

"No way!" she said incredulously. "Jake?"

Wendy chuckled and nodded as Bill grumbled down at the other end of the bar.

"It's not like I don't have enough to do running this place without having to keep an eye on the prettiest women in this bar. Now I gotta be waiter, bartender, and head bouncer of this joint." He leaned over and kissed Wendy on the head. "I'm used to having to watch out after this beauty, but now I gotta watch out for you three."

Wendy just playfully slapped her husband's shoulder, calling him an old coot. The girls laughed, but each coveted the love that was so obvious between Wendy and Bill.

"I want Tom and I to still have that in twenty years," Carol said with a dreamy look in her beautiful green eyes.

"I just want Rob and I to hurry up and get engaged so we can start that." Laurie declared, pulling her long brown hair up off her neck to cool off and then letting it fall back down her back.

Emma couldn't help but notice how much Laurie looked like Sarah. She smiled wistfully. Both girls looked over to Emma.

"What about you?" Laurie asked gently. "What about you and Jake?"

Emma smiled at the other women. "I'm in no hurry," she said honestly. "Right now I'm enjoying being the center of someone's world. Someone who makes me feel as though we have forever right now."

Hopping down from the bar stools the three women hugged closely. Making their way to an empty table, they ordered dinner. They talked, laughed, and shared for hours, never noticing the men who looked hungrily over at the three beautiful women.

Bill took his duties seriously, and whenever someone looked like they were circling their prey, he stepped in quickly. Soon all the men gave up, realizing that the three women were untouchable.

Looking up when Ted and a few other coaches from school came in, Emma's eyes followed them as they sat at the bar. He did not seem to notice her, but the bar was crowded. After about half an hour, he left and Emma felt herself breathe easier.

At one point, Emma noticed Wendy leaving the bar and walking into the back office. Emma excused herself to go to the bathroom. She made it to the office, unnoticed by Carol or Laurie, wanting to talk to Wendy privately.

Wendy looked up from the desk and smiled when she saw Emma. Emma glanced around the office, amazed at the pictures on the walls. The dark paneled walls were filled with shelves, loaded with photos of Brad and many of his sports trophies. Emma knew how proud Wendy and Bill were of their son, and she so hoped that whatever was happening with him would not jeopardize his future.

"Hey sweetie, whatcha need?" Wendy asked, looking up smiling.

Emma, not sure how to express her concerns just decided to jump in. "I've been concerned about Brad." Wendy looked confused for a second, so Emma plunged on. "His grades are slipping and I just wondered if there was anything going on that I could help with."

Wendy nodded in understanding. "Yeah, his dad and I have been on him lately. He seems so absent minded recently, not doing his chores or forgetting to do his homework. At first he just said he had too much going on."

Emma nodded, hoping the woman would continue. Encouraged, Wendy went on. "Bill called Brad's boss to tell him to cut Brad's hours when Brad wouldn't do it himself, but the shop owner told him that Brad had already cut his hours way back. When we confronted him, he got mad and said we needed to stop getting into his business." Wendy shook her head, lost in that memory for a moment.

"That was a bad night. We have *never* had a family fight like that. I used to hear people talk about teenagers being so difficult, but Brad has always been a model student and son. This really caught us off guard."

"What happened?" Emma gently probed.

"Well, after we all calmed down, Brad promised that he would bring up his grades. He apologized for lying about the job hours and just said that he was hanging with friends more since they would all be going to college next year and not get to see each other. He didn't tell us that he broke up with Suzy though. I had to hear about that from Bernadette." Wendy shook her head as she paused in thought.

"He's been better in the last week or so. He seems to be trying to be cautious about keeping his dad and me from being on him about things." Looking up at Emma, she smiled. "Just typical teenagers stuff, I guess."

Emma nodded and smiled back. Everything Wendy said had sounded very normal for teenagers. But for Brad to have such personality changes so quickly continued to make her suspicious. Leaning over, she hugged Wendy and promised to keep an eye out for him at school. Emma returned to the table to finish her girl's night out.

As the evening came to a close, the women headed out to their cars. Emma felt lighter than she had in weeks.

This is just what I needed. Food, fun, friends!

Reaching her car first, Carol turned to give each of her friends a close hug. Laurie and Emma walked over to their cars, arm in arm. Reaching Laurie's car next, they stopped to chat for a minute.

"So Em," Laurie said. "Are you happy with Jake? Is he everything you ever wanted? I mean, you guys seem great, but I just want you to be happy. You deserve everything, you know that don't you?"

"Oh sweetie, I am happy. Jake makes me happy. You make me happy. Being in this town makes me happy," Emma assured her. "I feel like I am home here with all of you." Hugging her niece tightly, she said goodbye and stepped away so that Laurie could get in her car.

Laurie waited until Emma had started her car, then she drove away. Emma started to back out of the parking space when she realized there was a piece of paper stuck under her windshield wiper.

I couldn't have gotten a ticket – I was in a parking space.

Getting out of her car, she walked around to grab the paper and opened it.

Oh no. Not another one.

Are you keeping quiet? Remember – no asking questions or your student will get hurt.

Emma quickly jumped back in, locked her car doors and started the engine again. She did not see anyone lingering around but she could not help but feel that eyes were on her everywhere. She pulled quickly out of the parking lot and drove home. Fear and anger warred within her, battling for dominance. She looked down at her hands on the steering wheel and saw them shaking. Even that made her angry.

How dare someone threaten me! How dare someone threaten a child!

Pulling into her driveway, she looked carefully at her house. The woods that in the light of day make her feel as though she is living in a fairytale forest, now seem dark and foreboding. Emma could imagine eyes peering at her from deep within the trees. The porch lights were still on and she could see her inside house lights lit as well. She had a clear view of the front porch and door. Looking carefully from the safe confines of her car, she could see nothing unusual. Feeling fearful, Emma jumped out of her car running to the front door with her keys in her hand.

She entered, quickly hitting the security alarm pad to re-alarm, shutting and locking the front door. Breathless, she leaned against the front door, willing her heartbeat to slow, as Mister swirled around her legs. As she stood there a moment, she remembered the last time she had been leaning against this very door. Was it really just a few hours ago she had been in Jake's arms, as he fucked her up against the door?

Shaking her head to clear her thoughts, she pushed herself away from the door and moved into her living room. Looking down, she saw she was still grasping the note in her hand. Taking a deep breath she sat down on her sofa and ironed the wrinkled paper with her hands so that she could read it again.

No asking questions

Emma tried to think of what questions she had been asking.

I asked about Brad. I talked to his teachers. I talked to Suzy. I talked to Ted. Maybe Ted talked to the other coaches? I talked to Wendy.

None of those people seemed likely to threaten her or a student, but at this point Emma was ready to consider anyone. She kept coming back to Ted. She hated to think that it could be him, but she couldn't reconcile all of the information that was swirling through her mind.

She decided to stop looking at the note, trying to decipher and find meaning in it. Folding it up, she put it in her bookcase with the other note. Emma wanted to focus on what she did know. Walking to her kitchen to grab a pen and pad of paper, she also started her coffee pot.

Another sleepless night.

Taking her writing utensils and her coffee, Emma sat at her table. She started to write down the facts that she knew.

1. Brad's grades are slipping. He is spending time away from friends and family. Lying about what he was doing.

2. Someone was seen in the park, near the old hut before the fire

3. Brad smelled like smoke.

4. 2 kids end up with heroin laced weed.

5. *Jake, Tom, Mike are working on drugs coming into area being sold to teens.*

6. *Ted doesn't want me upsetting Brad.*

7. *Ted doesn't want me looking into "his boys".*

Emma sat and looked at her list. She began to draw lines and arrows to what she thought was connected.

"Damn!" she cursed loudly. No matter how much she looked at it, she couldn't figure out how to connect the dots.

No wonder Jake is the detective, not me.

Thinking about Jake brought immediate guilt. Emma knew that he would be so furious to find out that she had hidden the threatening notes, but still was not willing to see anyone hurt. Stretching to ease her aching back, she put her paper away. It was now in the wee hours of Saturday morning and she realized how very tired she was. Knowing that Jake would be coming over later, she folded up her list and put it with the notes in the bookshelf. Checking the house one more time for safety, she took a quick shower before crawling into bed. Mister jumped on the bed, turning around a few times before settling in next to her pillow. She strangely felt comforted just by his presence, and drifted into a fitful sleep.

Chapter 14

The holidays were upon them, and Emma was excited to be spending it with friends. Mac and Bernadette had a small barn on their property that was close to the back of their house. They converted it years ago into a family rec room and at Thanksgiving they would invite family, friends, and any of the young firefighters who did not have family around. They had three picnic tables pushed together, plus several others brought card tables and chairs.

Laurie and Emma were out of school that week and went over to help Bernie set up. With green tablecloths on all the surfaces, splashes of yellow and orange fall mums on the tables, and pumpkins on hay bales, the place was transformed from a barn to an inviting Thanksgiving dinner scene worthy of Norman Rockwell.

On Thanksgiving morning, Jake came by to pick her up. Mary had already been picked up earlier by Mac so that she could help Bernie with the turkey. Jake let himself in with his key and heard singing coming from the kitchen. Walking in, he leaned against the door frame and watch Emma's hips swaying in time to the tunes coming from her ipod. Emma, not knowing Jake was there, continued to stir the green beans on the stovetop while singing and dancing to the tunes. Deciding to surprise her, Jake snuck in behind her grabbing her around the waist.

Emma screamed and kicked back with her legs, coming in contact with Jake's shins. He grunted in pain and felt himself falling backwards. The whirling dervish in his arms circled around and hit him solidly on the head with the wooden spoon. He fell backwards on the floor with Emma landing squarely on his chest.

"Goddamn girl," he grunted. "What the hell are you doing?"

"Jake!" Emma exclaimed. "Oh my god, you scared the daylights out of me! What are you doing sneaking up on me like that?" Her heart was pounding in fright, and she noticed the red mark on his forehead.

"Who the hell did you think was going to be coming into your house?" he said, holding on to her waist as she sat straddling him.

Emma blushed, knowing that she couldn't confess her fright from the recent threats and as a result was constantly on edge. Shrugging, she tried to joke,

"I guess I was just too involved in my new singing career." Noticing how scrumptious he looked in his tight jeans and black buttoned shirt, she decided that distracting him would be a good idea and certainly enjoyable for her.

Tossing the wooden spoon to the counter, she leaned over him until her breasts touched his chest. Touching her lips to his neck, she nuzzled and kissed her way around towards his ear, where she began to nibble. Jake groaned and slid his hands from her waist to her ass.

"Mmmm," Emma began to make noises as she continued to kiss his jaw, feeling his clean shaved face underneath her soft lips. Jake began to knead her ass and pressed upwards toward her crotch. Emma's lips made it back to his, and she began her assault. Jake let her take charge for a few minutes and then he angled his head for deeper access to her mouth. Tongues tangling, teeth clashing, Emma felt his kisses intoxicating her. She had started out to distract him, but she was now the one who could not think straight.

Sliding one hand under her skirt and into her panties, he stroked her wet pussy. Pushing two fingers inside, he began to circle them inside eliciting deeper moans from Emma. She began to rub herself harder on him, fucking his fingers. The pressure begin to build, and Emma could tell she was close to coming.

"Harder, Jake, harder," she groaned with her eyes tightly closed willing herself to slip over the edge.

"Babe, look at me," Jake ordered. Emma's eyes opened quickly and as soon as she looked into his face she felt herself go over. Jake felt her tight pussy grab his fingers as her orgasm washed over her. Emma lowered herself back down and rested her head on his chest, listening to his heartbeat as hers matched his, beat for beat.

"I love you Emma girl," he said gently stroking her back.

Emma raised her head up and smiled. "I love you too Jake."

Jake slowly pushed Emma back, and she made a mewling sound. "Emma, if I had my way, you'd be naked on this floor under me right now. But we promised Mac and Bernie that we would be there by eleven."

Emma looked up at the clock and saw that they only had a few minutes until they needed to go. Looking back down into his baby blues, she smiled a slow, calculating smile. She reached down and undid his pants. Jake raised his eyebrows at her.

"I think it's time I took care of you," she said slyly. Freeing his restrained cock allowing it to jut up proudly, she took it in her hands. Stroking up and down his length, she marveled at his size and the power she held in her hands. Emma leaned down, swirling her tongue around the head. Jake's head fell back onto the floor as he groaned, almost in agony. Emma slid her mouth down, continuing to swirl her tongue up and down as she went. His length was too large for her to take him completely, so with one hand she continued to stroke him at the base. With her other hand, she kneaded his balls gently.

Fighting the urge to fuck her mouth with abandon, Jake reached behind him to grab the edge of the counter. His hips began to move involuntarily, and he could tell he was ready to explode.

Letting go of the counter, Jake tried to pull her up saying, "I'm gonna come baby, you gotta stop."

Emma looked up into his eyes, but kept going. Jake felt his balls tighten, and he released in her mouth. He threw his head back, shouting," Fuuuuuuuuck!"

Swallowing several time, she continued to suck until she had the very last drop. Wiping her mouth with her hand, she looked at him smugly.

"Goddamn, woman. I can barely stand," Jake panted.

"Hmmm, Jake, I guess it's time we'd better get going or we're going to be late," she said smirking.

Jake growled as he quickly stood up, pulling Emma along with him. Hugging her tightly to his chest, he smacked her ass as he told her to get ready. Laughing, Emma fixed her clothes and grabbed the pot of beans off the stove as Jake straightened his jeans.

Emma had not enjoyed Thanksgiving as much since before her father, mother, and sister had died. The food was excellent, and the conversations flowed all around. She was enveloped in the warm feeling of being surrounded by family and friends. Rob helped his dad carry two turkeys from the kitchen, while Tom and Mike brought in the two hams. Jake pushed a cart that had sodas and water. Bill and Wendy brought the beer and wine, and Brad helped his dad while his mom assisted Mary to the tables. Laurie, Carol, and Emma made several trips bringing all the side dishes, and the five single firemen and policemen assisted Bernie with the rolls and pies.

When everyone was gathered around the tables, Mac rose to say the blessing. Holding hands with bowed heads, Emma could feel tears welling up in her eyes. Mac asked for God's blessings on everyone present and all the loved ones who were no longer with them. Emma discretely wiped a tear before it had a chance to fall. She felt Jake lean over and kiss the top of her head.

She heard him whisper "I love you, baby." She smiled and felt another tear begin to slip. This time, Jake took his finger and wiped it away. Emma felt loved. She felt comfort. She realized how long it has been since she had been surrounded by people who cared. Cared about each other. Cared about her. Emma felt at home.

~

Later as everyone was assisting in the cleanup, Emma found a chance to talk to Mike alone. "Mike, I've been wanting to ask if you found out anything about what was going on."

"I've been meaning to talk to you, Emma, but you are almost always with Jake when not at work," he joked. He looked into her eyes, and his detective training allowed him to see fear as well as concern. "Are you all right?" he asked.

"Yes," she lied. "I just wanted to know if you found out anything about the students or the coach or.... well anything."

"I can't discuss an ongoing investigation, but I can put your mind at ease. I did some digging but didn't talk to the student you were concerned about. I didn't think it would add anything new to the case."

Emma breathed a sigh of relief. She was glad that Mike had not talked to Brad. She had been so afraid he had been questioned, and that was the reason he had not been in to see her lately.

Jake, ready to leave, looked around seeing Emma in a private conversation with Mike. Jealously reared its head, but trusting Mike as a brother, he fought down the unfamiliar emotion.

Emma looked at Jake, realizing he was ready to leave, so she said goodbye to Mike and walked over to Jake.

"Hmm," he said. "I come in to take my woman home and to bed, only to find her deep in conversation with another man."

"Jealous?" she asked smiling up at him, while wrapping her arms around his neck.

"Should I be?" he asked, leaning down to kiss her on the nose.

"No baby. No reason at all. I am all yours. Always," she answered back, giving her lips over to his. Their kiss deepened until someone shouted for them to get a room. Everyone clapped and Emma looked up, blushing. She buried her head in his chest. Jake chuckled, and she felt his chest rumble. Looking over Emma's head, he caught his mother's gaze.

Mary was smiling, but Jake could see tears in her eyes. She had wanted Jake to find someone special for so long. She knew that Emma was the girl for him.

"*I love you son,*" she mouthed. Jake nodded at his mother and swooped Emma up in his arms.

"Happy Thanksgiving everyone. I'm taking my best girl home," he declared in a booming voice. The others cheered and clapped as he strode out of the barn toward his truck.

"Jake, you shouldn't have said that," Emma admonished, while inwardly smiling in satisfaction.

"Emma girl, you and I have a date with your bed!" he answered. And with that they drove back to her house to finish what they had started before dinner.

Chapter 15

Emma sat in her office, finishing the paperwork that was never ending in her job. With the seniors completing their college applications, she had to keep up with their transcripts. She looked down at the next application form on her desk. It was Brad Evan's. Thinking it would be a perfect opportunity to see him without appearing to be interrogating him, she sent a pass for him. A few minutes later, Brad entered her office cautiously. Looking up, Emma smiled at him and asked him to have a seat.

"I've got your application here. Let's go over it and talk about your essay and what else you need to get ready."

Brad relaxed and for the next twenty minutes, he and Emma enjoyed their conversation. He had a lot of questions, and she had the experience and knowledge to answer them. Emma realized how much she missed the times like this when she first moved to town, and Brad would come over to do yard work, then sit on her porch to talk when he was done. She knew she was taking a chance by moving the conversation to the latest events, but she needed answers.

"Brad, I need to ask you a question and I really hope you give me an honest answer."

He looked at her warily before replying. "What is it you want to know Ms. Dodd?"

Emma took a moment to gather her thoughts. She looked up, directly into his young eyes and began softly.

"Brad, the night of the fire on my property, a park ranger said that he had seen some young people in the park. The next day, when I saw you, you acted very strangely, and you smelled of smoke. I just want you to tell me if you were in the area and if so why. I don't care about the shed. I just care about you. If there is anything I can do to help, I want to help. I don't want *this...,*" she said as she laid her hand on his application, "to be at risk because you made some poor choices."

She sat quietly for a few minutes, letting Brad decide if he wanted to answer. He hung his head while she waited. Finally he looked up.

"Ms. Dodd, I like you. I have since I first met you. We really needed someone like you around here. Someone who cares. I just... I just don't...," he paused. He looked down at his hands as he twisted his class ring around and around. Taking a deep breath, he looked back up.

"You know, Ms. Dodd. It's time I manned up. I got caught up in some stuff that was making me crazy trying to figure out how to make it right. I broke up with Suzy because of it. I cut back my work hours because of it. I've lost sleep and disrespected my parents because of it." Brad sat up straight in the chair. "But no more. I don't want you to worry. I'm going to take care of it myself." He was looking directly at her, making eye contact, and she felt a mixture of pride and also fear.

"Brad, whatever it is, you need to let me help you. If it is illegal, then let me get Jake to help," Emma stated emphatically.

"No, not Jake," Brad said shaking his head.

Emma had an idea. "Well, if not Jake, then how about Mike?" Brad looked up at Emma with a confused look on his face.

Emma continued. "I'm sorry to tell you this, but after I smelled smoke on you I went to find Jake but he was out of the office. But Mike was there so I talked to him. He said he would do some discreet checking and if he did not need to question you, he wouldn't. He told me at Thanksgiving that he did not feel that he needed to dig further."

Brad nodded in understanding. "Maybe I will talk to Mike," he said. Pausing for a few minutes as though collecting his thoughts, he agreed, "Yeah, that may be just the thing I need to do."

At that he stood up to leave, this time turning to give Emma a hug again spontaneously.

"Thanks again, Ms. Dodd. I appreciate all you have done for me. Really, it means a lot."

Emma watched him leave, feeling better than she had in a long time.

∾

Emma and Jake had plans for dinner that evening. He called earlier in the day to say that he wanted her dressed and ready by seven, and he was taking her out on the town. Laughing, she asked him what she should wear.

"Emma girl, put on your best tonight. I'm showing off my girl," he replied.

Emma smiled as she hung up the phone. This day was getting better and better. She called Laurie as she was leaving the school. Laurie was known as the fashion princess and tonight she wanted to look her best. Emma knew Laurie would bring over some dresses since they were the same size, and maybe she could get Carol to drop by to do her hair and makeup. Excited to help, Laurie assured Emma that she would go home after work, grab some dinner dresses then head over to Emma's house.

As always now, Emma drove up her driveway, carefully perusing the area around. She preferred coming home in the daylight and nervously looked around at the area before getting out of her car. She had not received another note, but wanted to maintain diligence and not take any chances.

Her house appeared unaltered, so she entered and once again set the alarm. Mister, with his usual greeting of rubbing himself in figure eights around her legs, lifted his head as she bent to stroke him. Walking into her bedroom, she stripped out of her clothes, wanting to shower before Laurie came over. Stepping into the tub, she felt the pounding hot water ease her stress. After washing her hair, she shaved and lathered, knowing Jake loved her simple shower gel. Stepping out of the shower, she grabbed a towel and wrapped it around her hair. Grabbing another, she toweled off and then wrapped it around her body. Heading into her bedroom, she dropped the towel and slid into a short silky robe. Leaning over, she towel dried her hair, then ran her fingers through the tresses. Waiting on Laurie to arrive, she walked into her kitchen to pour a glass of wine.

A scraping noise near the back door startled Emma. She moved out of the kitchen toward the sound. With woods surrounding her house, Emma often saw raccoons, possum, and deer in her yard. She even found raccoons on her patio trying to get into her garbage cans, so she took extra precautions to place the lids on tightly to keep the critters out.

Oh, I don't have time to clean up their mess now.

Emma walked into the small mud room leading to the back door. A dark figure was on her patio, standing in front of the window. His face was hidden with a ski mask, but Emma looked on in horror as the figure was attempting to open the small window over the washing machine. She wanted to scream but found that no sound came out. She heard the sound of glass shattering and realized that it was not the window, but the wine glass that had slipped from her hands, splintering onto the floor. At the sound, the figure looked up at her, then turned and ran through the yard and into the woods.

Emma, startled into action, ran to the kitchen to grab her phone and call 911. As the operator came on, she finally found her voice, but couldn't seem to make coherent statements. She managed to choke out her address and "man outside", when the doorbell rang. Emma began screaming, terrified that he was now on her front porch. Through her screams, she heard a voice she recognized.

"Emma, Emma! Let me in! Emma!"

She recognized Laurie's voice and ran to the door. Throwing it open, she stumbled into Laurie's arms. Laurie grabbed hold of Emma and pushed her back inside. Laurie heard voices coming from Emma's phone on the floor, and she picked it up, quickly realizing that she had the emergency operator on the phone. Emma managed to calm enough to tell Laurie that there had been a man trying to break into her house. Laurie relayed that information and agreed to stay on the phone until someone came. Emma turned and seeing that the front door was still open, jumped up and slammed it shut. Hands shaking, she grabbed Laurie and pulled her into the hall, the only place in her house with no windows.

Laurie wanted to ask questions, but before she could get them out, the sound of sirens could be heard coming down the road. Laurie jumped up, looked out of the living room window and saw a cruiser come down the drive, followed closely by Jake's truck. The policemen jumped out with guns drawn, circling around the house toward the back while Jake and Tom came running up to the front door.

Emma threw open the door just as Jake reached it and jumped into his arms. He could feel his own heart pounding in fear as he held a shaking Emma in his arms. Tom pushed in around them, going over to Laurie.

"I don't know what happened," Laurie quickly explained. "I just got here and I heard Emma screaming before I could get to the door."

"What did she say?" Tom asked.

"She said a man with a ski mask on was on her patio trying to get in the laundry room window – the one by the back door."

Tom turned and looked at Jake, still holding a shaking Emma. He nodded at his partner and went toward the back to check it out. As he walked into the small laundry room, he noticed the broken wine glass on the floor. Stepping over it carefully, he made his way to the door and opened it. The patrolmen had made their way to the back yard as Tom stepped onto the patio. He looked to the right where the intruder would have been standing. Next to one of the bushes was a crowbar and a piece of paper nearby. Tom pulled his gloves on and picked up the piece of paper. He spoke to the patrolmen and had them begin securing the area.

He heard steps and turned, seeing Mike coming around the side of the house.

"Emma?" Mike asked.

"She seems okay. Shaken. Still with Jake and Laurie," Tom answered.

"What did you find?"

Tom showed him the note, now incased in a plastic bag. Mike swore and looked out towards the woods.

"It's not the first," Tom remarked. Mike just nodded.

"Jake is gonna be fucking furious," Tom continued. Mike just nodded again. The two men walked back inside of the house to head to the living room. As they entered, they noticed Rob standing in the doorway, holding Laurie. Knowing Rob, once Laurie called him, he would have broken all speed limits to get to her. Rob gave a head jerk in their direction and the men continued into the living room where Jake and Emma were sitting on the sofa, wrapped up in each other.

"Emma," Tom said softly looking over at his partner. "We need to talk."

Emma lifted her head from Jake's shoulder, her face tear streaked, and moved to sit beside him instead of on his lap.

Jake's heartbeat had calmed down slightly, but he was still so angry he found himself unable to process what was happening. *Get a fucking grip.* Jake forced himself to start thinking like a detective, not just a pissed boyfriend. He looked up at Tom and Mike, nodding that he was ready. As he turned to Emma, it dawned on him that she was wearing nothing but a robe. A thin robe. A short, thin robe.

Fuck, she is almost naked sitting here. Tom and Mike may be my friends, but they are still men.

"Laurie, take Emma into her bedroom and help her put some clothes on," Jake said quietly.

Emma, still in shock, just looked at Jake numbly. He took her face in his hands and gently pulled her face in close to his.

"Baby, you need to go with Laurie. She's gonna help you get some clothes on sweetheart."

Emma looked down, finally realizing her lack of attire and blushed. Clutching the robe around her, she stood as Laurie came over wrapping her arms around Emma's shoulders. The two women left the room as the other men politely averted their eyes, waiting until they were gone to begin speaking.

Chapter 16

"What have you got?" Jake barked out. Mike settled into one of the chairs facing the sofa and Tom sat on the coffee table close to Jake. Rob moved into the room as well, standing by the fireplace, wanting to know what was going on without interfering.

"We found a crowbar and this note outside the window of the laundry room," Tom replied handing the note to Jake. He watched silently as Jake read the note. He continued to watch as Jake's face began to show first his confusion and then his anger. He looked up at Tom, his jaw tight, enraged.

"She never told you?" Tom asked.

"You know she didn't," Jake bit back. "I sure as hell wouldn't have sat on this if she had." Jake stood up quickly. "Goddamn it!" he growled, running his hands through his hair, pacing the length of the small room.

Emma and Laurie entered the room again, Emma having changed into yoga pants and a simple t-shirt. She immediately felt the change in the atmosphere of the room and looked quizzically at the men.

"Jake, what is it?" she asked, walking over to him. He seemed so angry, but she needed his comfort. She reached up to touch his arm, but he swung around on her quickly holding out the note.

"You want to explain this?" he asked sharply.

Emma looked down at the note in his hands. It was like the others, only this one was encased in the protective plastic for evidence. The plain letters on the paper seem to scream out at her.

you are not taking me seriously – this is the last message I will leave – stop snooping and no one will get hurt

Emma's hands began to shake again, and she felt her legs give out from under her. Jake scooped her up before she hit the floor and settled her on the couch.

"Fuck!" Jake cursed.

"Jake," Tom spoke again, this time softly. "She needs you to be calm, man. Pull your shit together."

Jake, knowing Tom was right, took a deep breath. "Babe, I need you to tell me what this goddamn fucking note means. I need you to trust me."

Emma's eyes shot up to Jake's face. The face that kisses her so sweetly and whispers to her in the night. The face that calls her name when he comes inside of her. Now that face is so angry and his rage is focused on her. She could feel her chin begin to wobble, knowing tears were soon to follow.

Jake was aware of the change in her, felt her breathing hitch, and some of his ire release. Knowing that she needed reassurance he took her face gently in his powerful hands. "Emma girl, I'm not mad at you. I'm mad that someone is fucking with the woman I love. Someone has threatened you, scared you, and I didn't know that was happening. And a man like me, does not like to find out that his woman is being fucked over. So baby, we need to know what's goin' on."

Emma looked around at the room full of people, people that she knew cared about her. She had wanted to figure things out on her own and as much as she considered herself to be a strong woman, she was afraid. And now.... with someone trying to get inside her house, she was even more afraid. Looking down, she realized she was wringing her hands, trying to stop the shaking.

"Emma," Jake said again softly, knowing that she was still in shock. "Tell us about the notes."

Emma looked up into the baby blues that contained so much emotion; anger, fear, love. She knew she needed to trust that he would forgive her secretiveness and allow him to take care of her.

Taking a shaky breath, she plunged forward. "I've just…been…trying to pull the…puzzle pieces together," she started.

Jake looked at her in confusion. "Emma, I don't–" he started.

Tom interrupted, "Jake, let her finish."

Knowing that witnesses often need time to get all of their thoughts out in the open, Jake looked at Tom sharply knowing his partner was right.

Emma continued looking up at Jake, imploring him to understand. "Jake, I didn't mean to keep anything from you. I just wanted to find out what I could about the students and possible drugs in the county, and then I started getting warnings to stop."

"Warnings?" Jake growled.

Emma took a deep breath and then plunged into her explanation. "One day I came home and there was a cut up carcass on my front mat with a note, telling me to stop checking into things." She glanced at Jake and saw that he was about to explode. She quickly continued. "I then got another note left on my car the night that we had our girl's night out. At Smokey's, in the parking lot."

"Fuck!" Jake shouted as he jumped up. He paced the room, and Emma's eyes followed him around.

"Jake," Emma started.

"No Emma," he shouted. "There is no excuse for hiding this from me. Do you realize you could have been hurt? Do you realize that we may have been able to use these notes to further our investigation? Do you realize how stupid it was to keep this hidden?" His voice rose with each accusation.

Tears began to fall as Emma listened to Jake's rant.

"I had no choice," she said softly, barely being heard. Laurie started to walk over to Emma, but Rob held her back, knowing his friends needed answers.

Tom knew that Jake was in no position to be impartial. "Emma, what do you mean, 'you had no choice'?"

Emma looked down at her hands again. They were no longer shaking. In fact, she realized she no longer felt fear. What was coursing through her was anger. Anger that someone tried to take control over her. Anger that someone threatened another person. Anger that she was being blamed for the machinations of someone else.

Emma wiped her tears away and spoke clearly. "The other notes threatened a student if I told anyone."

Jake's head snapped around. "What?" he said with deadly calm.

Walking over to the bookshelf, she reached between two books and pulled out the notes. She handed them to Jake and stepped back as he, Tom, and Mike perused them.

Jake cursed once again and stormed out of the front door. Emma looked out of the window and watched him pace in the front yard.

Tom came over and pulled Emma into a hug. "He's not mad at you, Emma," Tom said. "He is just angry that someone was threatenin' you and he wasn't able to do anything about it."

Emma accepted the hug, then looked back out of the window as Jake continued to pace outside. "Should I go to him?"

"Give him a few minutes, darlin'. I promise it'll be okay." Tom stepped away from her, walked to the other side of the room and talked to Mike.

Laurie rushed over, enveloping Emma in a hug as they sat down together on the sofa. Emma felt drained. She leaned her head back on the sofa and wondered how her simple life had become so complicated. Mister coming back into the room now that it was calmer, jumped up on the sofa next to Emma, purring as he lay next to her.

Tom, Mike, and Rob walked out into the yard to talk to Jake. Laurie continually glanced over her shoulder to keep an eye on them as she comforted Emma. Looking at her niece, Emma thought how strange it felt to have Laurie caring for her.

As though she knew what Emma was thinking, Laurie grinned at her aunt, remarking, "You've certainly held me enough times over the years. It's high time I did the same for you."

Emma smiled and then took a deep breath. Straightening herself, she stood up saying, "Okay, enough feeling sorry for myself. I've got to start making this right."

The men had just re-entered the room when Emma made that announcement. Jake stalked over to her, grasping her by the shoulders and bending down to look directly into her dark brown eyes.

"Oh no, Emma girl. You are not doing anything else. Mike shared with us what you had talked to him about and while I'm not happy you didn't share with me, I get it. I also know you well enough to know that you're too stubborn to let this go and too caring to want to risk anyone else. So grab a bag and pack. You're coming home with me," Jake declared. Turning to Laurie, he asked her to help Emma pack.

Emma jerked out of Jake's hands, backing away. "Jake, I'm not going to be chased out of my house," she said emphatically, shaking her head.

The room erupted as everyone began voicing an opinion, the loudest being Jake as he reached back over to pull Emma into his arms. Her living room suddenly filled with testosterone pouring off of the four men, all wanting to protect her, seem to be devoid of oxygen. Claustrophobic, she felt light-headed. Emma sat on the sofa putting her head down between her knees.

"Guys. Stop," Laurie ordered as she plopped down next to Emma.

Jake squatted next to Emma. "Baby, what do you need?" Keeping his hand pressed to the back of her head, he gently rubbed circles on her neck. "Breathe, deep and slow. In and out, baby. Nice and slow."

Rob came from the kitchen with a glass of water, handing it to Jake. He helped her raise her head and held the water for her to sip. Color was slowing coming back to her face.

Emma gazed around the room, filled once again with the realization that these were people who cared deeply about her.

Finally, Mike's voice cut through the silence. "Emma," he said sharply to get her attention. All eyes went to him. "Jake is right. Right now, we are still investigating, and there is nothing you can do at the moment to help. You staying here in your home, could just hinder things – Jake won't be able to concentrate and whoever is behind all of this will probably come back."

Emma looked at the faces of the people in the room. Slowly Mike's words sunk in, and she realized he was right. She stood slowly with Jake's assistance.

Jake felt her shoulders sag in defeat. He pulled her in closer, willing his powerful arms surrounding her to be the shield that kept her safe. He rubbed his hands up and down her back, soothing her. *Please feel it baby. Please feel how I just want you safe. Please let me do this for you.* Shuddering, he tightened his grip. *I can't do this without you Emma. I need you. I love you. Please feel this.*

He felt Emma's arms tighten around his waist, and he dropped a kiss on the top of her head in relief. Emma pushed back just enough to look up into Jake's beautiful face. He was so tall, she had to look straight up to see into his eyes. Jake looked down into the eyes of the woman that had come to mean the world to him. *I will protect you darlin'. With my life.*

Emma held his eyes as she smiled a small smile that reached into his soul and wrapped around his heart. Breathing a sigh of relief, he leaned down and gently kissed her lips. Laurie walked over and took Emma's hand.

"I'll help you pack, Emma." The two women once again walked out the room, arm in arm towards the bedroom.

Tom came over and clapped Jake on the back. "We'll get him, Jake," he assured his friend and partner. Jake looked at Tom shaking his head in frustration.

"What are we missing, Tom? What is the missing link that ties this shit together?"

Rob's radio sounded as he was being called back to the fire station. Rob walked over to say goodbye to his friends.

"Let me know if you need anything, bro," he said. "Emma is Laurie's world and I love her too. I'll do anything I can to help." He shook Jake's hand and then headed back to the station after stopping in the bedroom to kiss Laurie goodbye.

Laurie left after eliciting a promise from Emma to call her if anything else happened. Tom caught a ride back to town with Mike after checking with the patrolmen who had finished searching in the woods. Jake, knowing that Emma would be worried about the cat, fed Mister and made sure he had plenty of water and a clean litter box. Taking a moment to stroke the now friendly cat, Jake assured him they would come back every day to feed him. "Don't worry, Mister. I'll take good care of your mistress." Mister looked up at the sound of Jake's voice as though to accept his promise.

Jake locked up the house, set the alarm, and settled Emma in his truck. The ride over to his mom's house was quiet.

Emma looked out of the truck window at what was left of the fall foliage. Most of the trees were bare except for the tall fir and pine trees. The woods were looking as desolate as she felt. Empty. Cold. Exposed.

Emma felt drained from the evening's events. She knew that she and Jake needed to talk but was grateful for the silence. She didn't have the energy to discuss the situation anymore.

∞

Mary was not surprised to see them; Jake had called her to say that Emma had an attempted burglary and needed a place to stay. Mary welcomed Emma with open arms and began fussing over her.

As independent as Emma was, she had to admit it felt wonderful to have Mary's arms around her. It had been so long since she had felt the comfort of a mother's touch. *What makes this different? What is it about a mother's hug that soothes? Feels different than other hugs? I miss you mom...*

Once again, Emma felt tears stinging her eyes. She allowed Mary to comfort her and show her to her room. Emma started to thank her, but Mary shushed her.

"Emma, sweetheart, it feels so good to be able to do something for someone," she said with a sad smile. "Sometimes I get so tired of others having to take care of me, it feels marvelous to do this simple thing." Mary hugged her and left the guest room. "Rest up, my dear."

Emma sat on the edge of the bed in the guest room looking around. The room was warm and welcoming. The distressed white antique dresser with a large mirror stood on the wall opposite of the window. Emma walked over to look into the mirror, shocked by what she saw. She had not bothered to put on any makeup nor styled her hair since she had planned on Laurie and Carol to fix her up. Red, puffy eyes in a pale face stared back at her from the mirror.

Turning away from the mirror, Emma walked back to the bed, sitting down on the soft lilac comforter. She listened to the sounds of Jake and his mother down the hall talking. She knew she should change out of her clothes, but suddenly felt as though every ounce of energy left her body. The shock had worn off, leaving in its wake an exhaustion whose pull she could not resist. All Emma could manage was to slide out of her yoga pants, leaving her t-shirt on. Pulling the covers down, she crawled into the comfort of the soft sheets and pulled the covers back up. Sleep overtook her and a few minutes later when Jake came into the room, she was sound asleep.

Jake slipped out of his jeans and crawled into the bed with her. He would never disrespect his mother's house, but it was Mary who insisted that he sleep with Emma.

His mom kissed him, saying that she was not so old fashioned that she would want to keep them apart, especially when they needed each other so much right now. Pushing him down the hall toward the room Emma was in, she surprised him. "Your father and I used to slip off together every so often before we were married, you know?" she said with a smile as he headed down the hall. Jake looked over his shoulder in surprise at his mom, but she had already turned to go into her room.

Leaning over Emma's sleeping form, he pulled her closer, willing her to be safe just by being in his arms. He thought of what this woman meant to him. He knew she was *it* for him. No other. She completed him, filled his lonely soul, and made him feel as though there could actually be a *'happily ever after'*.

Vowing to protect her with his life, he lay awake for several more hours, pouring over all of the possibilities of what he had learned. Finally, with one last kiss on Emma's head and with her tucked tightly into his body, he joined her in sleep.

Chapter 17

Over the next several days, Emma and Jake settled into a new routine. She rose early, assisting Mary as needed in the mornings before school and then Jake insisted on driving Emma to work. He always made time to pick her up afterwards and take her back to his mom's house. Emma wanted to argue that she could drive herself, but since Jake had not said one word to her about keeping the notes a secret, she decided not to rock the boat.

She loved having the opportunity to get to know more about Mary. Mary's rheumatoid arthritis was not debilitating at present, but Emma knew that she was taking some powerful drugs to try to combat the effects of the disease. Mary insisted on doing most things for herself, but accepted Emma's help when needed. Emma would assist with some of the housework and laundry, and also helped in the kitchen although she discovered that Mary loved to cook and refused to give that over completely. She and Mary would talk while working side by side.

Emma loved finding out more about Jake when he was growing up.

"He was always such a serious child," Mary acknowledged. "He loved to read, but he loved sports as well. Bernie and Mac used to live across the street from us, and Tom's parents lived down the street. Tom, Rob, and Jake were inseparable. And into everything!" she laughed. "The boys were very competitive, but in a good way. They supported each other and pushed each other to do better."

Emma found she could sit and listen to Mary's stories for hours. "And they went to the same college?" she asked Mary.

Mary smiled at the memory. "Jake had a football scholarship, and so did Rob. Tom played football in high school, but decided to go as a walk on when Jake and Rob settled on their school. They were good boys – caring, fun, but good students too."

"How did they all end up back in Fairfield? Isn't that kind of unusual?" Emma asked.

Mary's face had a faraway look for a moment, and Emma wondered if she should not have asked. Mary's face focused back on Emma, and she smiled, pushing her softly greying hair back from her forehead.

"Jake's father had a heart attack about the time he was finished with the police academy. By then I had been diagnosed with RA and the medicines were not at helpful back then as they are now, so Jake knew I might need some help. Jake never wavered – he came back here after graduating. Tom's parents had moved away by then, and Tom followed Jake to the police academy but took a job in another city at first. Rob always planned on coming back to work with his dad at the fire station. A couple of years later, Tom showed back up transferring to the Fairfield Police Department. He always said that life just wasn't as good without Rob and Jake around," she laughed.

Emma smiled at the thought of Jake being surrounded by family and friends. She understood – after all that was the reason she had relocated to Fairfield, to be closer to Laurie, her only family.

By then, dinner was ready and Jake had come in from the station. Walking in, his heart warmed as he saw Emma in the kitchen with his mother. Mary was still a very beautiful woman, slightly taller than Emma, and neatly dressed in slacks and a green sweater. Emma was simply dressed in black leggings and a long oversized red sweatshirt. As she reached up to assist his mother with something on a high shelf, he noticed how the skintight leggings made Emma's ass look mouthwatering. Right then, Emma and Mary began to laugh together, sharing a joke.

Jake couldn't help but smile as well. It made him feel comforted to see them get along so well.

Walking into the room, he kissed Mary on the cheek, then turned to Emma planting a big kiss on her lips. Giggling, Emma looked up into the handsome face of the man she loved more every day.

After supper, Mary decided to turn in early, so Emma and Jake piled up in the den to watch TV. Emma sat next to Jake with her legs tucked up under her.

"Jake," she started. "I was just wondering when I can go back home." She snuck a look up at his profile, seeing the set of his jaw. She quickly forged ahead.

"I love that your mom has welcomed me, and it has been great this week to feel safe and get to know her. But I miss my home, and nothing else has happened and I just really want to be back at my own house." Emma knew she was talking fast and rambling, but she hoped the she could get it all out before Jake answered back. "Please baby, I just want my life back," she finished softly touching him gently on the arm.

Looking down at the small hand resting on his arm, he reached over and covered her hand with his much larger one. Raising his eyes up to her beautiful face, he was struck with how vulnerable and yet how strong she was. He always felt as though he was walking a tightrope of wanting to protect her and yet knowing that she was strong and independent on her own. He never wanted her to feel smothered, but protected. Sometimes, he had to admit to himself, it was hard to tell the difference. Sighing, he turned, gathering her in his arms.

Emma melted into his embrace. She loved sleeping in the same bed with Jake at night, but with Mary across the hall, they had not made love since she had moved in. She loved their closeness but missed their intimacy. As she sat on Jake's lap, she could feel his erection pressing into her hip. She moved to get more comfortable, and he moaned and grabbed her hips to still her. Emma giggled and nuzzled his neck.

"Emma girl, behave," he ordered.

"I know baby, I just miss you," she whispered.

He pressed little kisses on her neck leading up to earlobe, and she began wiggling again. They both pulled away at the same time, knowing they needed to stop. Jake maneuvered her back onto the sofa, and he moved himself to sit on the coffee table facing her. He leaned in, holding her hands in his.

"Hopefully it won't be much longer. We are making some breaks in the case. The kids who OD'd, were able to tell us who their buyer was, and we are followin' that chain. Our assumption is that your threats didn't come from some students, but someone higher up that drug chain who feels as though you're gonna find out something while you are just doin' your job. That makes them dangerous babe," Jake continued.

"I know," Emma said disheartened.

They sat quietly for a few minutes, Emma lost in her own thoughts, and Jake carefully watching her, wanting to keep a pulse on her emotions.

"We never got our night out," Jake reminded her. "How about we try that again tomorrow?" Emma looked up and smiled. "We can even make it a group if you want. We could get the gang together at Smokey's".

Emma laughed. "Hmm, will it be like the first time we met at Smokey's? I'd hate for you to be there with the old lady date!"

Leaning back, he groaned at the memory. Standing, he scooped Emma up and tossed her over his shoulder. Quietly slapping her ass, he growled, "Babe, if you can be quiet, I'll take you to bed and show you what I think of my 'old lady'!"

Emma laughed again and promised to be quiet.

Jake proceeded to make love to Emma as quietly as possible, and Emma found herself pressing her mouth into her pillow several times to stifle her moans and passionate screams. She fell asleep an hour later, blanketed in Jake's massive arms feeling loved and protected.

Next door, Mary just smiled to herself.

Emma talked Jake into taking her home the next day to pick up some more clothes and to get ready to go out with the gang. Jake made her wait on the front porch as he went in first, checking every room.

"Jake, hurry! It's freezing out here." Emma found herself thinking she was glad her house was small so it wouldn't take long to check. Jake came back quickly to the porch to let her in. Emma looked around the living room, feeling satisfied it was just as she had left it. Somehow, she imagined that someone would come back to trash her house. Greeting Mister, she immediately fed him, stroking his fur.

Walking into the kitchen, Emma opened the refrigerator.

"Babe, what are you doing?" Jake called from the living room. "We're eating at the bar when we get there."

"I'm checking to see what needs to be thrown out. You've been coming over to feed Mister and I haven't been here. We left in such a hurry last week, I've got strange things growing in here," she replied as she began throwing out some food that had spoiled.

Jake walked into the kitchen and was greeted with the sight of Emma bent over as she looked in the bottom drawers of her refrigerator. Losing focus on everything else, he concentrated on how delicious her ass looked. All he wanted to do at that moment was have her naked in that same position, with her hips in his hands as he took her from behind. As the blood rushed to his dick, he felt his jeans getting that familiar tightness that always seemed to be present when she was around. Emma stood up and turned around.

Seeing Jake's expression, she laughed. "Are you checking out my ass?" she asked.

"Oh hell, who gives a shit if we're late," Jake proclaimed and walked over and picked Emma up. She immediately wrapped her legs around his waist. He plopped her down on the counter. Diving in for a kiss, his lips were commanding, and his tongue demanded entry. Jake was in a take charge mood, and Emma loved it. He angled his head to deepen the kiss, plundering her mouth as though it had been forever since he explored it. Emma found herself breathless as she grasped his shoulders to hold on.

Jake slid his hands from her ass up her sides to the undersides of her breasts. There he let his hands cup the fullness of her breasts, feeling their weight. Emma moaned in his mouth and tried to press herself closer. Jake grabbed her ass again and jerked her to the edge of the counter where his erection could press into her hot pussy. Emma reached out and began pulling on his shirt, pushing it down off his shoulders. Jake stepped back just enough to slide Emma's t-shirt up over her head, their lips separating only for the second it took for the material to pass by. Feeling as though she were drowning, she didn't care if she ever took another breath on her own again. Jake hands slipped behind her and unclasped her bra, sliding it off her body. The weight of her breasts fell, and his hands moved back around to massage them, tweaking and pulling on her nipples.

Emma felt herself growing wet, and she began to squirm against the counter looking for a release from the pressure building inside. Jake dropped one massive hand and placed it on her thigh effectively stilling her.

"Oh no, baby," he said. "The only way you're getting off tonight is with me."

Emma reached down and unbuttoned his pants, sliding the zipper down his huge cock. Sliding his boxers down as far as she could reach, she took him in her hands. Warm, silky, firm. She began stroking him gently at first then with more pressure. A pearl drop of pre-cum appeared on the head, and Emma swirled it around with her hand. Jake's kisses left her mouth and traveled down her neck into her cleavage. He wrapped his warm lips around one nipple, pulling it deep into his mouth. Emma threw her head back as the sensations spread from her nipple straight to her core. Jake went from nipple to the other, laving them, worshiping them, then he continued kissing his way south until his head was forcing her legs apart. Using one hand to gently force her to lay down on the counter, he began to lick her folds before plunging his tongue in deeply. Emma's hands were grasping his hair as she felt the pressure build. Seeking release, she begged Jake for more.

"Jake please… please just take me… I am so close," she moaned.

Jake looked up at the beautiful woman spread out in front of him, not believing that she came into his life and vowed to bring her pleasure for the rest of her life if she would have him. Smiling at her moans, he lowered his head back to finish the job he started. He continued to lick and suck until Emma was on the precipice. Jake moved up just enough to suck hard on her clit. Screaming his name, Emma went over the edge.

Emma lay back on the counter, in a blissful orgasmic coma. Jake stood and slipped his jeans and boxers all of the way off and kicked them to the floor. Picking Emma up, he carried her to her bedroom and gently laid her on the bed. He lay on top of her, resting his weight on his arms and began to kiss her again.

Emma grasped his cock in her hand, placing it at her entrance. In one swift movement, Jake buried himself deeply inside her wet pussy. Emma gasped with the fullness of him.

Jake moved back and forth slowly at first, building in speed until he was pounding in Emma. "Grab the headboard baby." Too lust filled to pay attention, she kept her arms around him.

Jake stopped moving. "Eyes babe," he ordered. Looking directly into his baby blues, she once again realized he was in charge tonight. "Get. Your. Hands. On. The. Headboard. Now."

She raised her hands above her head, grabbing onto the headboard then quickly felt Jake pounding in and out again.

"Spread your legs farther."

This time Emma immediately followed the order, knowing her pleasure was first and foremost on his mind. The pressure building again as the friction increased. Body tingling, sparks centering in her core seeking release.

Reaching down to massage her breasts, Jake pinched her nipple.

"Jake, I'm close," she screamed. Jake pulled out quickly, and Emma felt the loss immediately, moaning in disappointment.

He flipped her over on her stomach ordering, "Up on your knees baby." He gripped Emma's hips in his strong hands and entered her again thrusting as far as he could push. This position changed the sensation and Emma quickly felt the familiar explosion as she went over the edge again. Jake continued for a few more forceful strokes until he felt his cock strain and climaxed, jerking and releasing into her waiting body. He collapsed onto her back, feeling numb in ecstasy. Both breathing heavily, Jake soon rolled to the side to take his weight off of her tiny frame. Emma continued to lay on her stomach with her head turned to face him.

They lay for a while, facing each other, saying nothing but feeling everything. Sometimes, Emma thought, words aren't necessary. All she needed was right here beside her in the bed. This magnificent man who showed her more and more each day what it is to be cared for. She basked in his love, stroking his arm, looking into his baby blues. Jake rubbed his palm along her back, over the globes of her ass and back again.

Her cell phone chirped with a message, and they quickly looked at the clock, then back at each other.

"We're late!" Emma cried as she started to jump from the bed. Jake pulled her back down on top of him, hardly feeling her weight. He held the back of her head and pulled her in for a deep, but soft kiss.

Emma relaxed into the kiss. Slowly he released her, smiling up at her beautiful face.

"I love you, Emma girl," he whispered. Looking down at this handsome, caring man, Emma smiled back.

"I love you too, Jake," she replied. "Always," she added gently.

Chapter 18

A cold front moved in and a pre-Christmas snow was predicted. It was the week before the holidays, and the students were anxious to be out.

"My students are bouncing off the walls," Laurie complained. "You should be glad you are at the high school."

Emma laughed. "What makes you think teenagers are any better than your first graders? They are just as excited, only bigger!"

Laurie had called Emma before school, checking to see what she and Jake were doing for Christmas.

"I guess we will be with his mom," Emma answered. Laurie heard the wistfulness in her voice.

"You miss your house, don't you?" Laurie asked.

"Yeah. Don't get me wrong. Mary is great. But I so wanted to decorate my house for the holidays and have people over. I have now been out of my house for two weeks, and I am going crazy," Emma replied. "Oh, the first bell is ringing and I have hall duty. Talk to you after school."

Emma was back in her office later, when Brad asked if she could see him.

"Sure, come on in," she greeted. It had been a few weeks since she had talked to him. Looking at him closely, he appeared nervous and yet was making eye contact. "What's up?" she asked casually.

"Ms. Dodd, I need to you tell something." Emma sat quietly, giving Brad the opportunity to talk at his own comfort level. "The night of the fire, remember? At your house?"

Encouraged, Emma nodded willing for him to continue.

"Well, I was near there," he paused but then quickly added, "but I didn't start it."

"Okay," Emma said gently. "Can you tell me what did happen?"

Taking a deep breath, he plunged on. "Me and the guys go to the park, down by the little river, kind of on the back side of where you live now. We discovered it last summer." He looked back up at Emma, with a guilty look. She sat quietly, waiting for him to continue.

"We found that it was a good place to umm... party, you know?" He blushed a little, as though he was embarrassed to be admitting that he partied. Emma gently smiled at him.

"We liked it because it was back over that ridge, and the Park Rangers never go down there and well, until you moved in, there hadn't been anyone living on your side of the river in years. We could play music, drink beer, and sometimes take our girlfriends there. When it was warm, we would even swim some 'cause the water wasn't too fast at all." Brad chuckled. "We used to wonder why they called it a river when it was more like a big creek. I know that is why our grades were slipping at the beginning of the year. Senioritis hit and we just wanted to party." He looked back up into her eyes and stated firmly, "But we NEVER had a fire there, I swear."

He paused again and then continued. "We knew it was illegal to have fires in the park and we just never wanted to take a chance on doing something that stupid."

"What happened the night of the fire?" Emma prodded.

"It was only me and a couple of guys hanging out drinking. We heard some noise across the river, and we started to walk over. We started seeing some flames, and the other guys ran off." He looked away, an expression of embarrassment crossing his face.

"We knew we could get in trouble being out there drinkin'." He raised his eyes back to hers. "I ran over the log connecting the two sides and saw someone near the flames of the hut. Smoke was coming out, and the flames were shootin' up. I couldn't get a good look at who was out there, but he turned around and saw me. Ms. Dodd, I'm ashamed to say, I took off runnin' too. I hightailed it back over the log and caught up to my friends. I didn't say anything at first – no one was hurt and I just went home."

"Brad, you could have told me. We could have told the police. Drinking in the woods with your friends isn't a good thing, but I know your parents would want to know that you were safe. Jake and your parents could have helped out. What were you afraid of?" she asked.

Brad shook his head slowly, eyes misting over. He raised a hand up, pressing his fingers into his eyes trying to keep the tears from falling. Emma quietly leaned over and pulled a tissue out of the box on her desk, holding it out to him. He took it gratefully, wiping his eyes. Then he looked back at her, straightening his back. Emma waited until he was composed enough to continue.

"What happened then, sweetie?" she asked gently.

"The next mornin' I told my friends that I was going to the police. They're good guys, Ms. Dodd. We were all scared but we were all going to go together. When we got to my truck after practice, there was a note on the windshield. It was a warnin'."

Emma's blood ran cold. *Oh my God. Brad's been threatened too.*

"The note said that I was to stay quiet or they would make the evidence look like we did it and I'd lose my scholarship. Me, Scotty, Rick, and Nate all just looked at the note and froze. Ms. Dodd, I'm not afraid to tell you we were scared shitless," he said emphatically.

"I'm sure you were. I would have been too," Emma confessed. She looked at him wonderingly. "What's changed now, Brad? Why are you telling me this now?"

Brad sat quietly for a few minutes, pulling his thoughts together. He raised his teary eyes up to hers.

"I just heard my parents talkin' about how you've been gettin' notes too and how someone is tryin' to get to you. They said you'd been chased out of your house. That's just not right, Ms. Dodd. I thought about it all night and decided it was time to man up. I talked to the boys this morning. They know I am here. They agree."

Emma reached over and placed her hand on his arm, smiling at him. "Brad, keep this in mind before you beat yourself up too much. It is not the measure of a man in the mistakes you make. But in how you choose to correct those mistakes."

Brad glanced up into her smiling eyes and found himself smiling back. He felt lighter than he had felt in months. Taking a deep breath, he asked her what they should do now.

Emma thought for just a minute. She told him that she would call Jake and let him know what was going on. She also said she would call his parents and talk to them as well. She was going to tell Wendy and Bill to come pick him up after school and have them with Brad when he gave his statement to the police. Brad nodded, seemingly relieved for the first time since he came into her office. She stood as he did, pulling him into a hug.

Looking into his eyes, she smiled and said, "You did good, kiddo." He just nodded and left her office.

Emma sat back down, feeling better than she had in a long time. Pondering the new information, her mind began to race with ideas.

Finally, we may be getting somewhere. Who would have wanted to burn down the shack? The only reason would have been if there was something there that they did not want anyone to know about. That property had been vacated for years so the hut in the woods would have been the perfect place to hide something. And when I moved in, it may have made someone nervous. I know the police checked out the area and didn't find anything. But maybe, something was missed.

Grabbing her phone, she called Jake. His phone went straight to voicemail. She left a message that told him to call when he got a chance. She then called the station to see if Mike or Tom was available. The dispatcher put her through to Mike.

"Hey Emma, what's up? You finally decide to dump Jake's ass and give me a chance?" Mike joked.

Emma laughed. "No, but if I ever do, I'll let you know," she joked back. "Listen, I wanted to let you all know that Brad Evans and his parents are coming to the station right after school. He and some guys were near that old hut that burned and he may have seen something suspicious."

"What did he see?"

"I want him to tell you himself, but I will just say that he saw a suspect at the time of the fire. It seems that he and some of his friends ran but then got a threatening note to not tell anyone. I wanted to talk to Jake because I was going to head back over to my place and see if there is anything suspicious still there."

"Don't be foolish, Emma," Mike admonished. "You know Jake would shit if he knew you were off by yourself over there. We didn't find anything and determined it could have been a vagrant that had used the property because it had been vacant for so long."

"I know, Mike. But what if there is something there. A vagrant wouldn't threaten Brad's scholarship if he told anyone."

There was silence on the phone as Mike pondered this information. "You're right, Emma. But I don't want you to go. How about if I drive out there myself, check things out again. You could come in here to the station, wait on Jake, and be here when Brad, Wendy, and Bill get in."

Emma had to admit that Mike's plan made sense. She agreed, hung up, and then realized the last bell had rung. Looking out of her window, she saw Wendy and Bill picking up Brad. She called them earlier, knowing this was going to be hard on them, but they were proud of Brad for coming forward. Reaching for her purse, she checked her cell phone noticing that Jake had not yet returned her call. Walking to her car she glanced over when she saw Coach Ted jogging to his truck. As she was driving through the parking lot, ready to head to the station, Ted peeled out leaving her to stare after him.

Did Brad tell the coach what he was going to do? Why else would he be heading out of here as though his ass was on fire?

Quickly changing directions, Emma decided to head over to her place. She would be safe if Mike was over there, and she didn't want to waste any time. She tried Jake's cell phone again but he still didn't pick up. Calling the dispatcher, she was told that Jake and Tom were already in the interview room with Brad and his parents.

"Just tell him that I have headed over to my place to check out the burned hut with Mike. I have some suspicions and want to check them out." She didn't want to mention Ted's name; she had no proof that he was involved in anything illegal and wanted to be careful what she said.

Seeing that Ted was traveling a few cars ahead of her, she wondered if she should follow him instead of going to her place. Her decision was made a few blocks away when she was stopped by a red light. She lost track of Ted, but didn't care. By now she convinced herself that she needed to be with Mike looking over the burned area. Pulling into her driveway, she followed the familiar curves until her house came into view. Even in the dead of winter, the sight of her house warmed her heart. She couldn't help but smile, determined to put an end to whatever was keeping her from enjoying her home. Driving toward the garage, she parked outside. Stepping outside of her car, a blast of cold air swirled around, showing that the temperature had dropped significantly. Leaning back in, she grabbed her scarf. Shoving her keys in one pocket and her cell phone in the other, she started off around the house.

Tromping over the dead grass she thought back to the activity of last summer; Brad mowing, Helen planting flowers, and Jake coming around to see what needed to be worked on.

More determined than ever, she headed into the woods at the back of her property towards the Little River. The last time she had been in the woods it was fall and there were still a lot of leaves on the trees, full of red, gold, and orange. Now as she walked, she noticed how desolate everything looked. Winter was not her favorite season. The wind kicked up and she wrapped her scarf tighter around her neck.

She found herself attempting to walk carefully and quietly, but had no idea why. It was as though she instinctively felt fearful, without knowing what there was to be afraid of. She desperately wished she had either called Mike to see when he would be here or that she had waited on Jake.

Emma stopped suddenly at the sound of voices raised in anger. Her heart began to pound as she wasn't sure what to do. Peering ever so slowly around the large tree that was blocking her sight, she tried to discern who was in the woods near the river. She could see two men, but only one was partially visible.

"I'm done, you hear me? I'm out," one of the men said.

"You'll be done when I say you're done. Nothing's changed. We've got a good deal here and it works because you don't ask questions, you just do what I goddamn tell you to do."

"No more, I'm telling you. I've sat back and watched my boys be scared, but no more," the first one shouted again.

My boys? Oh my God, that's Ted.

Placing her hand on the rough bark of the tree in front of her to keep her balance, she leaned farther around the edge to see if she could identify the other man. She could see Ted facing in her direction, with his hands up.

"Come on man, put the gun away," Ted said nervously.

Emma's eyes searched the ground for something she could use as a weapon, but she saw nothing. Just then her pocket vibrated, and she realized someone was calling her cellphone. She quietly slid her hand into her pocket and pressed accept call. Looking down she saw it was from Jake. *Please let him hear what is going on.*

Chapter 19

J ake and Tom finished interviewing Brad with his parents. Handling himself like a man, Brad gave clear answers and held nothing back. Wendy and Bill, were anguished that they had not tried harder to get their son to open up to them when they noticed his personality changes. They had chalked it up to teenage hormones, never realizing how much of it was due to the stress that he felt.

"Mom, Dad, you did nothing wrong – it was all me. I made stupid choices and then got scared. Coach even told me not to worry about it."

Jake, Tom, Wendy, and Bill all looked at Brad incredulously.

"Coach? You told Coach Ted, and he said nothing?" Bill said, anger showing in his voice.

Brad looked around at the faces all staring at him, and he nervously admitted, "Yeah. I told coach right away, when I first got the note to stay quiet. He agreed and told me that the best thing I could do for everyone, including you and mom, was to stay quiet and pretend nothing happened."

Wendy and Bill exploded in a flurry of cursing and threats. "Goddamn, son of a bitch, wait till I get my hands on him!" Bill threatened. Tom calmed them down and made them promise not to say anything to anyone until it could all be investigated. Wendy and Bill reluctantly agreed. Leaving, with their arms around Brad, they thanked the detectives for handling everything.

After they left, Jake looked over at Tom. "That son of a bitch works with Emma and knows she has been talking to the kids," he cursed.

"Do you think he is the one who left Emma the notes?" Tom asked.

"I don't know, but I sure as hell am going to find out."

"Not alone, partner. I can't have you go off halfcocked and ruin this investigation." Tom threatened.

Jake turned and stared his partner in the eyes. "And what if it were Carol that were being threatened?" he asked. "Would you back off then?"

Tom stared right back at him, grim faced at the thought of someone ever harming his wife. "No." Then he smiled at Jake. "But I sure as hell would want my partner at my back."

Jake nodded his head firmly. "Damn straight. Let's go."

Striding out of the interview room, they grabbed their coats to head out the door. Sally, the dispatcher, called them back.

"I've got a message from your pretty lady, Detective Campbell."

Turning back around, Jake pulled out his cell phone, noticing several missed calls from Emma. He started to call her back when the Sally continued her message. "She called earlier and talked to Mike. He headed out later to say he had to go check something out. Then Ms. Dodd called back to say that she had planned on being here with the Evans when they came in, but she decided to go out to find Mike. And she was....hmm, now what did she say exactly." Sally shuffled through some papers quickly. Jake was already dialing Emma's cell as Sally came up with the note.

"Oh yes, she said she was following someone suspicious from school and would try to meet up with Mike's investigation."

The Chief of Police walked over to Jake, looking confused. "Why the hell is your Emma following someone suspicious?" he bellowed.

"I don't know, but I sure as fuck am going to find out!" Jake swore again.

Right then Emma picked up her phone.

"Emma, where the hell are you?" he roared. All he could hear was muffled sounds, and he gave Tom a questioning look.

"Put her on speaker," Tom said wanting to hear what Emma was saying. Jake hit speaker as he, Tom, the Chief, and Sally all leaned in to listen more closely.

At first, Jake could just make out the sounds of two people arguing in the distance. His heartbeat began to pound as he realized that wherever Emma was, she wasn't able to talk right at that moment but she must have wanted him to hear what was going on.

❧

"I could shoot you now and dump your ass in the water. Or drag you over to the park and let the animals take care of you. So you got a choice. You either keep quiet, keep bringing those drugs over in the athletic buses from games, and you can keep living. How about that, you prick?"

"I never meant to get in this deep. I thought it was a time or two. I never meant for you to burn down this hut getting everyone suspicious. I can't keep doing this to my boys."

Jake and Tom looked at each other. "Ted," they both said at the same time.

The chief turned to Sally. "Put out a call, I want everyone looking for Ted Williams and get Mike on his radio or cell phone. He is off somewhere, and we need to know if he knows where Emma Dodd is."

Right then, they heard a gunshot and a scream.

"Mike, you son of a bitch, you shot me!" they heard Ted yell. There was a pause and then he screamed again, "Emma, NO!"

Another shot rang out.

Chapter 20

Blood pouring from his leg, Emma saw Ted go down. He looked up and cursed at Mike then saw her behind the tree. He tried to warn her away, and that was the last thing he was able to do before being shot again. Mike whirled around, gun still in his hand.

"Emma, you stupid bitch, why didn't you stay away?"

Dumbfounded, Emma stared at the scene in front of her.

Mike? Mike? How could he be involved?

Looking at the gun in his hand, pointed directly at her, she felt fear trickle down her back in a way she had never known before. She wanted to run but was paralyzed at the sight of the gun.

"Goddamn, you are fucking up my plans!" he screamed.

"What plans?" Emma asked softly, thinking only to calm him. She had forgotten the phone in her pocket recording the scene like a bad movie script. Mike rubbed his hand over his face, then seemed to come to a decision. He walked over and grabbed her arm as she tried to back away.

"Come on, I gotta get rid of his body and then we're going to take a little walk. Then I am going to simply lose you in the park, in the cold and dark. The chances of you getting out are minimal. That will give me time to get away, and everyone will still be looking for you and not me." He held on to her upper arm tightly and started to drag her forward. He stepped over Ted's body and pulled her over it when she hesitated. Emma tried not to look at Ted, but she had to see if he was still breathing. He was perfectly still, eyes staring open in death.

"Oh my god, you killed him!" Emma could feel the bile rising, and she flopped forward and began to throw up. Mike threw her on the ground in disgust. As soon as she stopped retching, he grabbed her arm again and hauled her to her feet.

"Roll his body down the embankment," Mike ordered, swinging the gun wildly in the air. Emma stood in shock, not moving. Shoving her in front of him, he ordered her to move Ted's body again.

"I... I... can't. I... can't," Emma repeated, shaking her head, tears welling in her eyes.

The crack of Mike's hand slapping her across the face sounded out in the silent woods. Her body jerked to the side with the impact of the blow. She brought her shaking hand up to touch her stinging cheek, feeling the wetness of tears streaming down her face.

"Emma, you do it now, or I will kill you here and bury you with Ted!" Mike shouted.

Terrified, Emma felt her legs give out as he forced her down on the ground next to Ted's body. She tried to roll him, but his weight was too much. Frustrated, Mike grabbed her arm again and shoved her away. He rolled the body over the river embankment out of sight, while keeping his eyes on Emma. Still kneeling in the dirt, she wanting to run but could not seem to get her trembling legs to stand.

Finished with Ted, Mike trained the gun back on Emma as he stalked over to her. Grasping her bruised arm once again, he pulled her up and pushed her in front of him.

They walked to the edge of the Little River where an old log lay across it. Hesitating at the end of the log, she turned around to see what he wanted her to do. Mike used the butt of the gun to push her forward.

She tentatively placed her foot on the log, then stumbled across the distance over what she remembered Brad had referred to as a big creek. Perhaps it seemed narrow to teenagers playing in the summer, but Emma tried not to look at the swirling water rushing below her.

As they reached the other side, Mike ordered her to move forward a few steps and then told her to stand still. Turning around he pushed the log to the side, so that it fell into the water.

Emma wanted to run, but the gun trained on her back kept her following Mike's orders. The wind blowing stronger, sent shivers through her. Her hands were cold, and she slid them into her pockets to keep them warm. As she did, she felt her cell phone.

Oh my God, I forgot the call from Jake. Oh please let him have been listening.

With new resolve, she decided to see if she could get Mike to talk just in case Jake was still on the phone.

"I don't understand Mike. What did Ted mean by the athletic buses?"

"It was the perfect set up. My contacts in the pipeline needed an easy, undetectable way to keep the heroin coming into the area. One night Ted and I were at Smokey's, just drinking and shooting the shit, when he mentioned that part of his job duties was that he had to arrange all the buses for the athletic teams when they travel from one county to another. God, it was so easy – the idea just came to me that night," Mike bragged.

Emma kept her hand in her pocket, trying to hold the phone up in a way to maximize the chance that Jake could hear the conversation. She stumbled over a root and went down on her knees.

"Get up. We don't have time for you to be stumbling every step." He looked over at her. "Why are your hands in your pockets?" he asked.

"My hands are freezing – I'm just trying to keep them warm." It was only a partial lie as she could feel the cold seep into her fingers as well as her toes.

"Girl, you are going to feel a lot colder before this is over."

"Where are you taking me?" she asked, hoping he had a destination in mind that could be relayed to Jake.

"My Jeep is up here over this next ridge. I'm taking you on up the mountain and getting rid of you there. I'll have time to get back to town, circle around, and join the search for you." He chuckled, congratulating himself on his grand plan. "It won't be too hard to get everyone off the trail."

"Why did you burn down the old shack back there," Emma asked, turning around to look at Mike's face. His face darkened.

"Goddamn, you really have screwed things up since you landed here, you know that?" he growled. "No one has lived there for years; it was the perfect place to hide the stash when it came off the buses. Once I got Ted involved, my contact would get the drugs into the equipment bags on the buses while the teams were in the locker rooms. After the kids got home, Ted would bring the bags to the hut and lock them up. I would get them the next day and get them out to my southern contact. Goddamn, it was perfect. Then you moved in, and I had to try to keep you from wandering around your property."

Remembering the times that Mike had warned her about the woods and vagrants, Emma remembered he convinced Jake that she didn't need to walk around check out her acreage.

The landscape around them became steeper, and Emma was having a hard time walking. Her toes ached from the cold, and she was shivering under her coat. The wind picked up more, whipping her hair about her face. The woods were thick, bare limbs and underbrush scraping her hands, face, and legs as she stumbled along. Whenever she would stumble, Mike would curse and prod her with the gun again.

She looked back at Mike and was shocked to see that he seemed impervious to the cold or strain of climbing, as he continued his diatribe.

"The last drop I made, I wanted to make sure that there was no evidence in case you started looking, and I heard those kids across the river watching me. I knew I had to get rid of all evidence permanently so I set it on fire." He chuckled to himself again. "I even stayed behind to handle the fire investigation after making sure that Jake was caring for you."

Emma was astounded – Mike had been in the perfect position to make the contacts, cover evidence, even to make threats to keep everyone in line. And no one would suspect him. She even thought of him as a friend.

And Jake. Oh my god. This will kill him to think she was kidnapped by his friend. Fellow detective. A brother. A psychopath.

By this time, they were making the last climb to the top of the ridge. The cold had seeped in as Emma realized once again how poorly she was dressed. Her knee length skirt, stockings, and heeled boots made for poor hiking attire she thought ruefully. Her stockings were torn, and her knees were bleeding where she had fallen several times. She looked up and saw Mike's familiar Jeep. She didn't know if she was relieved or terrified.

"I've never been in the park this far up," she said, hoping against hope that her phone call was still connected. "Where are we?" she asked.

Mike laughed and answered, "Hawks Ridge. But we're heading up higher, darling. We're heading to Bear's Ridge. Can you guess why it's called Bear's Ridge?" He continued to laugh as he prodded her once again with the gun, moving her next to his jeep.

Emma whirled around on him, stopping short as he raised the gun back to her face. "You bastard!" she spat.

"You know it babe. Hands behind your back," he ordered. Mike put his handcuffs on her and pushed her into the back seat of his jeep before jumping into the front. Starting the Jeep, he drove up the winding road higher into the park's mountains.

"You never finished telling me why you are doing this?" she continued to prod.

"Do you know how much new detectives make in this podunk town?" He looked in the rearview mirror, and Emma shook her head. "I made good money working as a cop in the state capital. Found how easy it was to take a little from the drug busts. Hell, I was livin' good for a while. They got suspicious, but I was never accused. Things got a little hot so I decided to move on to a smaller town and see what I could do to make some money on the side."

"So all this is about money?" Emma asked, her voice quivering with fear and anger.

"Haven't you heard, Emma? Money makes the world go round," he chuckled at his own joke. "And there is a lot of money to be made this way. Stupid kids don't care what shit they get high off of as long as they get high."

Emma thought back to the two students who had heroin in their weed. "You get them hooked, on more than just pot!" she said incredulously. "You get them hooked so they keep coming back to your sources."

"Don't be so high and mighty, counselor," Mike said looking back at her in the rear view mirror. "I don't force anyone to take anything. Those kids put that shit in their own bodies, no one makes them," he rationalized.

Emma had dealt with teens and addiction before, but she had never been faced with the blatant cruelty of a drug supplier before. "You prey on the young! You may not force it down them, but you make it so available and easy. You make them need it, and then you make them need you. You're….. despicable!"

Mike laughed. "Is that the best you can come up with, Em?

She wanted to scream and rant but looking into his cold eyes staring back at her, she knew nothing she could say would ever make a difference to him.

Emma looked outside, noting that the sun had dropped below the tree line, deepening the shadows of the woods all around them. Night was falling fast and so was the temperature.

Oh Jake, where are you? Will you be able to find me in time? I just want to tell you one more time that I love you. I want to look in your baby blues and tell you that you hold my heart in your hands. She felt a tear slide down her face. *What will Laurie do if I don't come back? She has lost everyone. Oh god, please let Rob take care of her. Let her know that I would never willingly leave her.*

The jeep came to a jerking stop, and Emma bounced forward, slamming her cheek on the seat in front of her. Jolted out of her morbid musings, she looked out. It was now pitch dark. Her heart pounded as Mike jumped out of the jeep and came around to her side. He pulled her out and turned her around to un-cuff her.

"Can't have your body found with my handcuffs on it, now can I?" He pulled her over to the top of a steep ridge, looking down on what Emma could only assume was more woods.

"Not gonna shoot you either. Don't want any evidence at all. By the time anyone finds what is left of you, it will just look like you had wandered, got lost, and perished. Perished... that's sounds like a nice way to die, doesn't it? Emma perished in the cold mountains." Mike chuckled again at his own sick joke.

Emma looked at him realizing that what sanity he had, was completely gone. She looked back over her shoulder, trying to figure out what to do when there were suddenly tremendous noises and lights coming towards them. Mike, surprised, grabbed

Emma and pulled her in front of him. Her heart pounding, she could feel her shaking legs giving out.

Disoriented, Mike began shouting and cursing waving the gun round then pressing it up against Emma's temple. A state police helicopter flew around the side of the cliff and shone its spotlights down on them. She and Mike both threw an arm up to shield their eyes as he jerked Emma tightly to keep her in front of his body. The only thing keeping Emma on her feet was Mike's arm around her waist and the pressure of the gun against her head.

The noise and lights from the helicopter camouflaged the sound of police cruisers coming around Mike's jeep.

DROP. YOUR. WEAPONS.

Whirling around, keeping Emma in front of him, Mike was enraged. Cursing, he tightened his grip on her.

Jake walked in front of the police cruiser, its headlights illuminating behind him, looking like an avenging angel. He stalked forward, approaching the couple on the edge of the ridge, with his gun pointed at Mike. Tom circled around to the side. The area began to fill with police, park rangers, and Rob and Mac leading the rescue crew.

"How... how did you find us?" Mike asked, keeping his gun pressed to Emma's head, with his other arm wrapped around her chest. Jake said nothing, but pulled his cell phone out of his pocket and waved it back and forth. Mike looked on in confusion, then suddenly jerked Emma tighter to him.

"Bitch! You have a cell phone on you. You god-damn bitch!" he screamed, pressing the gun tightly to head. "I ought to kill you right now!"

The police chief spoke softly, "Mike, give it up son. It's all over. I've got men who have found Ted's body, we've talked to the boys that were at the hut, we've got your confession on Jake's cell recorded for the past hour. It's over now. Let Emma go, Mike."

Emma began to shake. She knew Mike wasn't in control of his mental stability right now, and she wasn't even sure he was listening. With the bright lights behind Jake, she couldn't see his face or expression. She just focused on the massive shadow outline of the man she loved.

"No, no, it's not supposed to end like this." Mike's arms jerked Emma back closer to the edge of the ridge. Holding the gun tightly to her temple, his breathing ragged, he began to grin slowly.

"Hey Jake," Mike called out. Jake looked sharply in their direction, showing no emotion. Heart pounding, he focused on the prey in front of him holding his revolver steady.

Come on fucker. Jake thought. *Come on. Just move slightly to the side, and you're a dead man. Emma, just hold steady. I got you, baby.*

"Looks like I got your girl in the end, doesn't it bro? Well, if I'm not getting out of this, she's not either!" and with that Mike backed up and hurled himself off the edge of the ridge while still holding on to Emma.

"Noooo!" Jake roared, as he saw the woman he loved being pulled over the edge.

Emma screamed and felt weightless for an instant as they flew through the air before the impact of hitting the ground jarred her. She and Mike rolled over and over, down the incline, rocks cutting into them, tree limbs tearing at their clothes and skin. Their bodies separated, and Emma came to a stop when she crashed into a boulder.

Stunned, she lay slowly losing consciousness. She was afraid to move, not knowing what might be broken. Her body was screaming in pain, and she could feel tears falling down her face, but couldn't move her free arm to wipe them away. Far away she could hear her name being called.

She was cold. So cold. She could still hear her name being called but it wasn't getting closer. It was farther and farther away, drifting off on the howling wind. Closing her eyes she first felt horrible pain, then eventually fear, then finally peace. She could see her mother's beautiful face. Behind her mother, was Sarah, smiling.

I'm coming home mom. I'm so cold and hurt, and I just want to see you again. Take me home mom. I'm coming home......

～

Jake came crashing down the incline, heedless of the danger.

"Emma! Emma!" he yelled over and over. Tom was right behind him, stumbling down the side of the ridge. Rob followed with a medical backpack, and another rescue crewmember had the ropes and stretcher board. Stumbling upon Mike first, they could see his head was at an awkward angle having broken his neck during the fall.

"Goddamn bastard, rot in hell!" Jake choked out.

The rescue team member radioed back to the top that there was a fatality, quickly assuring them that it was Mike and not Emma. They would need to send down a body bag. Chief and Mac looked at each other, both praying that there would only be one body bag needed.

Jake continued down, cursing the dark, swinging his powerful light back and forth. The spotlight from the helicopter scanned the area where they were desperately searching, illuminating shadows and shapes.

"Jake, over there!" Tom exclaimed pointing to a large boulder to the right. Jake scrambled over, seeing a small unmoving body pressed against the rock.

God no, no! Not Emma, not when I just got her in my life. God don't take her now.

Jake went to gather her in his arms, noting her battered body.

"Don't touch her!" Rob ordered. He moved over and checked her pulse. Looking up at Jake and Tom, he said, "She's alive. Barely."

The rescue team came down, stabilized her neck and back, then placed her in the carrier. Carefully hauling her up the mountainside, she was loaded inside the ambulance. Jake jumped in with them, daring them to try to kick him out. The ambulance headed to the hospital; Tom called Carol and Rob called Laurie. Carol was already at the hospital and Laurie was on her way.

∾

The hospital waiting room was crowded with a large number of Fairfield residents. Rob sat, comforting a distraught Laurie, while Bernie and Mac took the seats next to them. Mac's arm was around his daughter Suzy's shoulders. Bernie had brought Mary to the hospital and she sat with her head bowed in prayer. Helen and Roger came as soon as they could, closing up the hotel's lobby for the first time in years. Brad stood with his parents, stoically trying not to cry, while Bill had one huge arm around him and the other holding Wendy tightly against his chest. Various policemen, firemen, teachers, and students all passed through the waiting area, checking for news, offering comfort, and just needing to feel the closeness that comes from shared grief.

Tom looked around at the crowd of people, all there for one tiny powerhouse of a woman who had touched their lives in such a short period of time. He looked over at Jake, standing off to the side with his head in his hands, knowing that Jake was unaware of anyone else at the moment. Tom kept hoping that Carol would come back in and update them as she had been for the past several hours. Crossing the room, Tom stood next to Jake, placing his hand on his partner's shoulders. He could feel Jake's body shake with emotion.

The double doors swung open and a doctor in surgical scrubs came out, with Carol right behind him. Jake jerked his head up as Tom's grip tightened on his shoulders.

"Family of Emma Dodd?" the surgeon asked to the crowd.

"I am," Jake and Laurie said at the same time. Looking at each other for a second, they wrapped their arms around each other and Laurie corrected, "We are."

The doctor proceeded to list Emma's injuries while Jake's head felt as though it was spinning with all of the information. He could feel Laurie's legs wobbling and was glad for the support as Rob approached and took hold of Laurie. He heard words but couldn't fit them all together. Contusions, fractures, dislocated shoulder, concussion, internal bleeding, coma …the words just kept coming. After the doctor finished, he asked if there were any questions.

The only thing that Jake could manage to get out was, "Doc, just tell me, is she going to be okay?" Since the internal bleeding was stopped with the surgery, the doctor's main concern now was the possible brain injury with the swelling and concussion. "Only time will tell," he concluded. "We're watching her closely." With that, he shook Jake's hand and headed back down the hall.

Jake, numb, just stood staring at the doctor's back. Carol, who had walked over to support Laurie, reached out and gently lay her hand on his arm.

"Jake, as soon as they get her settled in ICU, you and Laurie can go back. I'll take you when you are ready."

Jake and Laurie walked with Carol down the long sterile hospital hall. Each room they passed, Jake glanced in seeing other ICU patients and their rooms filled with anxious faces. Each one with their own story, their own pain, their own hopes, their own grief. As others turned their faces to him, he saw understanding. When his father had been ill, Jake realized he had been too young to truly understand the human emotion of shared grief. Seeing his emotions mirrored on the faces of others in the hospital, he knew he wasn't alone.

Holding tightly to Laurie's hand, not knowing if it was for his support or hers, they entered Emma's room.

Chapter 21

The lights were so bright, but they did not hurt her eyes.

There was a golden glow all around, like the reflection of the sun setting over the ocean.

That perfect moment when the last of the sun's rays cast brilliant colors over the moving water, and everything has a pastel crystalline beauty.

Emma's mother was on the shore, the pearlescent light glowing around her face,

and Emma could feel herself floating toward her.

Her mother opened her arms, wrapping them around Emma as she stood before her.

Emma, surrounded by her love.

Home. That was where love was. She remembered their home.

The laughter, the sharing, the love. That was home. Emma looked up into her mother's wise eyes and saw love shining from them.

I want to go with you, mom. I've miss you so much.
I'm ready.
I want to go home.

Oh Emma dearest. This isn't your home. Not yet.
It's not your time.
You still have so much love to give. You still have a
home to fill with love.

Emma pulled back and looked around, not
understanding.

You, my precious child, you will be home with me
someday, but not right now.

Emma's mother began to slowly move away. Emma
reached out for her,
but she could no longer touch her mother's arms.

Mom, mom, don't leave me again…

Emma dearest, it is time for you to go to your home.
It's time for Emma's home.

Harsh. Bright. Glaring. Emma was aware of the light, but this time causing pain instead of comfort. She felt herself floating, but could not hear peaceful shore sounds. Only sharp beeping and the sounds of murmuring. She forced her eyes to open, not understanding where she was. She still felt as though she was floating, but her body was not moving. Trying to turn her head, she couldn't seem to move it on her own. Emma cut her eyes over to the side and saw Jake slumped in a chair, his face unshaven, hair uncombed, shirt wrinkled, eyes closed.

As her fog-filled mind began to clear, she remembered the events leading to her going over the mountainside. She remembered looking at Jake right before Mike pulled her over and realizing that all she wanted in life was to be with this man every day, in every way. She loved him with a love that was boundless, endless, forever. She wanted to build a home with him.

Home… Home.

She remembered. A tear slid down her face as she remembered her mother. Was it a dream? It doesn't matter. Her mother came when she needed her and guided her, just as she always had. That was what her mother meant. She was meant to build a home here, with Jake.

Emma smiled. A home with their children.

Thank you mom. Thank you.

Emma closed her eyes again in the peaceful sleep of one who knows they are loved.

The next time she opened her eyes, Jake's beautiful baby blues were staring back at her.

"Hey," she said softly.

"Hey back," he said smiling. He reached his hand around and cupped her bruised face gently. This time the tear that slid down was on his face.

"Oh Jake, honey don't cry. I love you," Emma said with reverence.

Tears continued to fall from Jake's eyes. "Emma girl. I thought I lost you. I thought I was never going to have the chance to tell you that I want to spend every night watching you sleep and every morning watching your beautiful eyes open. I want you in my life every day. Every way."

Emma smiled up at him. "Jake, I saw momma." He looked at her in confusion. "When I was sleeping," she continued. "Do you want to know what she told me? She told me that it was my time to build my home here. Jake, I choose you. You're my home."

Jake leaned over and touched his lips to hers in a tender, love filled kiss. "As soon as you're out of here babe, we'll make that home. I promise. Wherever we are together, that will be home."

Epilogue

Four months later

J ake waited at the end of the aisle in the small white church on the edge of town. His dark suit fit perfectly, having been made just for him. The color set off his sandy blond hair, which had been trimmed recently. The jacket of the suit was cut to fit his wide shoulders and arms. The white shirt underneath and bright blue tie stood out starkly against his tan skin. Jake's eyes scanned toward the back of the church, hoping the ceremony would start soon. His gaze found his mother's face, as she smiled up at him.

Proudly standing next to Jake was Rob and Tom, equally as handsome in their dark suits. Tom leaned over. "Nervous?"

Jake shook his head and smiled. "Hell no. Been waitin' for this for a long time. Ready to make it official."

Rob just grinned as Tom nodded in agreement.

Emma stayed in the hospital for ten days until she was stable enough to go home with Jake and Mary. It had taken a couple of months of intensive physical therapy for Emma to be able to walk with a cane and regain full use of her arms. The bruises on her body healed much quicker than the bruises in her mind. Nightmares still occasionally plagued Emma, but when they occurred, Jake held her tightly until they subsided. Emma and Mary had grown inseparable, assisting each other as best as they could.

Suddenly the back doors of the church opened and the three men straightened, making an impressive sight. Carol walked down the aisle first, wearing a blue strapless, knee length dress, showcasing her delicate features and blonde hair. Tom smiled at his beautiful wife as her eyes sought his. Laurie followed next, in a similar dress as Carol's only with a strap over one shoulder. Her long brown hair hung down her back in soft curls. Rob's eyes never left the beautiful woman that he was lucky enough to call his own. He winked at her as she crossed in front of him to take her place.

Jake anxiously waited to see Emma, suddenly now nervous. She appeared at the back of the small church and began to walk down the aisle. Roger, looking as proud as a real father, escorted her as they began their slow journey towards the waiting groom. The continued physical therapy allowed Emma to walk with just a slight limp, but she was wearing ballerina flats instead of the heels she had so wanted to wear.

Jake's breath stopped momentarily as his eyes took in the vision that was moving towards him. Emma's hair was swept up, partially hidden by her ivory veil, with tendrils framing her face. Her ivory dress was a flowing creation of silk and lace, with a sweetheart neckline that just showed a hint of the top of her breasts. Emma was wearing the pearl earrings and necklace Mary had given to her the week before.

Her deep chocolate eyes were sparkling, but it was her smile that rocked Jake's world. As she kept her eyes on his baby blues, her radiant smile lit her entire face and he could have sworn he felt it right down to his very soul. As Roger placed her small hand into Jake's much larger one, Jake drew her close to his side. Smiling down at her, he leaned over and whispered, "I love you, baby."

As Emma and Jake exchanged vows, the emotion was so palpable that the congregation wiped tears from their eyes as they witnessed the union of two souls destined to be together. As the minister declared them to be husband and wife, Jake picked Emma up in his powerful embrace lifting her in the air, kissing her as though his life depended on her as his next breath.

"Forever, Emma girl?" Jake softly asked, looking into the eyes that held his soul.

"Forever, Jake," Emma replied, tears of joy sliding down her cheeks.

Four Years Later

Emma slowly opened her eyes, seeing her handsome husband sleeping next to her. She never tired of staring at his face. A face that could break out into a smile that made her breath catch, a face that could hold her in ecstasy as he pleasured her long into the night, a face that could gentle with the holding of his child.

Speaking of his child, Emma could hear cooing coming from across the hall. She quietly slipped out of bed, stopping to rub Mister, sleeping on the bed at Jake's feet. Walking across the hall, she looked down at their beautiful daughter playing in her crib. She scooped her up, snuggling her close. After changing her, Emma carried her back into their bedroom, holding her tightly as she slid back into bed.

Feeling the bed move, Jake opened his eyes to the most beautiful sight any man can wake to. He looked into the deep brown eyes of his wife, nursing his baby girl. A girl that had her mother's dark hair and chocolate eyes. Baby Sarah looked at her dad's face and reached out to pat his cheeks. Jake pretended to bite her chubby fingers, and Sarah burst into baby giggles. The door bounced open with force as three year old Richie came running into the room, sending Mister scrambling off the bed. Emma looked at her son's rumpled sandy blond hair and baby blue eyes, seeing a younger version of her husband.

Jake made room for his son as he climbed into the bed. The four of them sat, quietly snuggling for a few minutes, until Richie's enthusiasm for starting a new day was too much to hold in. Laughing, Jake grabbed the little boy, saying, "Come on, son. Let's go get dressed."

Emma looked up, mouthing *Thank you* to Jake as he took their rambunctious son off to get dressed so that she could finish nursing Sarah. In a little bit, they all headed downstairs for breakfast.

"Gamma, gamma," Richie said.

Emma looked at her son and told him that he could run get his grandma. Jake watched as Richie ran from their house across the yard to where his mother, Mary, now lived. Stepping out on the porch with his coffee, he looked around in satisfaction. Once Emma was released from the hospital four years ago, they decided not to waste any time and immediately began to plan for the future. He still remembered seeing her walk down the aisle, taking his breath away. Hearing his son's excited voice, his attention was pulled back towards the yard, where Richie and his mother were walking together.

He and Emma had her old unused garage torn down, and they built a bigger house next to her little one. A house big enough for kids, he told her. As it was being built, they equipped her original house with some features that would make moving around easier for his mother. As soon as both houses were finished, they moved in. Emma would never consider not having Mary move with them. Now, Mary had a one level house that fit her needs and Jake's growing family had their own home.

The sun was now peeking through the fall leaves of the woods surrounding them. The colors of fall were glistening in the early morning sunlight. The autumn morning mist was burning off, leaving the crispness in the air that only fall can bring. Emma walked outside carrying her coffee.

"Sarah?" he asked, looking down at his beautiful wife.

Emma smiled. "Your mom has Richie eating his cereal and Sarah in her bouncer. She's happy. They're happy. All's great for the moment," she joked.

Jake wrapped his powerful arm around her, pulled her in closely and tucked her tiny frame into his. Looking into those eyes he could drown in, he leaned down and kissed her forehead.

"Emma girl, do you have any idea how much I love you?" he asked. "I never thought I would find someone so perfect, so giving, so loving. You are my life, darlin'. You and those children, are my whole life."

Emma looked up into Jake's strong face. "Jake you are everything to me. Everything I thought I might never have, you have given to me. You're my family, my life, my love…. My home."

Jake set their coffee cups on the porch railing and pulled Emma around to his front. Touching completely, he leaned down and captured her mouth in a soul searing kiss. Soft and gentle, sweeping his tongue into her mouth, catching her moan with his. Emma raised up on her toes and met his tongue stroke for stroke. They slowly separated, his heated eyes noticing her kiss swollen mouth. Emma's eyes opened to see his piercing blue ones staring deeply into hers and her smile shined on his world.

"Think grandma will keep the kids later on?" he asked huskily, adjusting the crotch of his pants. Laughing, Emma assured him that she thought his mother would love to watch the kids for a while. Right then, Ritchie's shrill voice could be heard, calling for his dad. Smiling, Jake gave one more quick kiss to Emma's lips.

"Love you babe. Love those kids. Love this home," he said as he gathered their coffee cups.

"Love you too, honey," Emma said tucking herself back under her husband's embrace.

Arms around each other, they turned to walk back inside to their waiting family. Back inside… to Emma's home.

The End

The Fairfield Series continues with Laurie and Rob's story. Here is the beginning of their story.

Laurie's Time

Book Two of the Fairfield Series

Prologue
Laurie (age five)

Laurie's mother watched her play on the swings in the city park. Laurie's long brown hair would fly out behind her only to sweep back into her face with every movement of the swing. Higher and higher she would go, her giggles catching on the breeze as her mother looked over at her five year old daughter. Sarah leaned back, letting the spring sun warm her face, smiling at her Laurie's obvious happiness. Laurie had certainly not been a planned child, but Sarah loved her fiercely, as a lioness watches over its cub.

"Mommy, mommy!" Laurie called as she came running over. Sarah gathered her precious child in her arms.

"I love you, baby girl," Sarah whispered in her ear.

"Will you love me forever?" Laurie asked as she looked into her mother's beautiful face.

Kissing Laurie's forehead, hugging her tightly, she replied, "I will love you forever."

Sarah sat with Laurie napping in her lap. Sarah's mind took a trip down memory lane to Laurie's father. Sarah had just turned sixteen years old and one of her best friends convinced her to go to out one evening when her parents and sister were out of town. While Sarah had never been one to take chances, she felt the need to break out of the constant good girl image that everyone had of her. They went out that evening and managed to slip into a crowded bar across town where no one would know them.

Swaying to the music, Sarah was completely unaware of the effect she had on the men around. A petite brunette, with long shiny waves down her back, she had curves in all the places that makes a man sit up and take notice. Her beautiful face, with minimal makeup, made her look almost fairylike; the type of woman that would also make a man want to protect. Dressed simply a light blue sundress that was not designed to be sultry at all, surrounded by other women dressed for sex, she was one of the most beautiful women in the bar. And Brock Sinclair noticed.

Brock was a young soldier, between tours in Desert Storm, in town visiting with some of his Army buddies. They decided to hit up one of the neighborhood bars for a night of drinking and hooking up. Brock, who had a busty redhead sitting on his lap nuzzling his ear, had been drinking steadily ever since they arrived at the bar. Knowing he was going to get lucky with … well, he didn't know her name but with the tits on the redhead, he didn't care what her name was. A few more beers and then he planned on taking the redhead back to the hotel he was staying in a banging her until the sounds of artilary no longer rattled in his dreams.

Sarah and her friend had just entered the bar and Brock had noticed the natural beauty the moment she walked in. Suddenly, the idea of the screwing the fake titted redhead, wasn't as appealing as the vision standing near the bar looking nervous. A strange sense of protectiveness washed over Brock and he instinctively knew she was not old enough to be in the bar. Looking around, he realized that he was not the only man noticing the beauty.

"Wouldn't mind tapping that ass tonight," said the buddy next to him.

Growling in answer, Brock stood up, effectively dumping the redhead in his lap, saying, "Here, you need a piece of ass? I'm sure this one will do. She won't care which soldier she fucks." And true to his

296

prediction, the redhead stood up grumpily at first, then turned to his buddy and began nuzzling his ear.

Brock walked over to his princess…. *his princess? Where did that thought come from?* Shaking his slightly inebriated head, he continued over to Sarah.

Sarah felt a presence behind her and she slowly turned around. Looking up, she stared into the grey eyes of the most handsome man she had ever seen. Tall and slender, he had dark brown hair cut in a short military style and a face that would have filled every one of her teenage dreams.

They talked for several hours and then Brock took her back to his hotel room. Sarah knew she shouldn't go with him, but she trusted him and found that she wanted him more than anything she had ever wanted. Brock never asked her how old she was making the assumption that she was at least eighteen. As the evening progressed into the wee hours of the morning, they kissed and fondled until they were both so engulfed in lust, they gave in to their desires. Jake was slow and caring, although not realizing that she was a virgin until it was too late. They fell asleep in each other arms, Brock dreaming of his fairy princess and Sarah with her handsome prince.

Sarah woke early to the knocking on the door. She slipped out of the bed and opened the hotel door, having put on Brock's Army t-shirt first.

Recognizing one of his buddies at the door, she told him that Brock was still asleep. The buddy just looked her over and told her to hit the road. Looking confused, Sarah just stood there immobile.

"Look babe, we got shit to do today and Brock don't never like waking with one of his hookups hanging around. So take off quietly and have a nice life." With that, Brock's friend headed back to the room across the hall.

Sarah, confusion melding into embarrassment, turned and looked at Brock as he lay tangled in the sheets. Realization that she was a one-night stand rushed over her and she couldn't wait to leave before he woke up and further burst her bubble. Quickly and quietly, she dressed and looked at him longingly one last time before leaving, grabbing the t-shirt before she shut the door. She just wanted to have something to hold as she remembered this night.

Brock woke up, reaching for the beautiful girl sleeping beside him only to find her gone. The evidence of their lovemaking was left on the sheets so he knew he had not created her in a dream. Brock was furious when his buddy explained that he had gotten rid of the girl and vowed to start looking for her. But the call came through – their leave was being cut short and it was time to head back to base.

He never knew that nine months later his princess gave birth to his daughter. He also never knew that twelve years later his princess was killed in a car accident, leaving their daughter an orphan.

Acknowledgements

First and foremost, I have to thank my husband, Michael. Always believing in me and wanting me to pursue my dreams, this book would not be possible without his support. To my daughters, MaryBeth and Nicole, I taught you to follow your dreams and now it is time for me to take my own advice. You two are my inspiration!

My best friend, Tammie, who for eighteen years has been with me through thick and thin. You've filled the role of confidant, supporter, and sister. My hometown cheerleader, MyckelAnne – you've been my partner as I figure out what I am doing and keeping all my secrets!

Going from blogger to author has allowed me to have the friendship and advice of several wonderful authors who always answered my questions, helped me over rough spots, and cheered me on. To Kristine Raymond (my first supporter – I still have our long emails saved) you gave me the green light when I wondered if I was crazy and never let me give up. To my other amazing author friends, A.D. Justice, L.L. Collins, Andrea Michelle, Ann Vaughn, the amazing authors of the Indie Round Table, and to the indie author community – thank you from the bottom of my heart.

My beta readers kept me sane, cheered me on and are now reading the second book in this series. Thank you to Kristine, Denise, Cindy, Noelle, Jennifer, Tera, Miranda and MyckelAnne. My street team is so supportive, promoting this book and me as an author. Thank you Denise, Cindy, Noelle, Jennifer, Tera, MyckelAnne, Danielle, Shannon, Andrea, Chelle, E.J., and Victoria.

As the owner of the blog, Lost in Romance Books, I know the selflessness of bloggers. We promote indie authors on our own time because we believe fully in the indie author community. I want to thank the many bloggers that I have served with this past year, continue to serve with, and who are assisting in promoting my series.

Most importantly, thank you readers. You allow me into your home for a few hours as you disappear into my characters and you support me as I follow my indie author dreams.

Author Information

Maryann Jordan

I am an avid reader of romance novels, often joking that I cut my teeth on the old bodice rippers. I have been reading and reviewing for many years. In 2013, I created the blog, Lost in Romance Books to promote and showcase indie authors. In 2014, I finally gave in to the characters in my head, screaming for their story to be told. The scene in Smokey's where Jake and Emma first meet was a scene in my imagination for several years. From this musing, Emma's Home was born.

I, like Emma, am a high school counselor having worked in education for thirty years. I live in Virginia, having also lived in four states and two foreign countries. I have been married to a wonderfully patient man for thirty two years and am the mother to two adult daughters. When writing, my dog or one of my four cats can generally be found in the same room if not on my lap.

Please take the time to leave a review of this book (on Goodreads, Amazon, Barnes & Noble). Reviews are the lifeline for indie authors.

Feel free contact me, especially if you enjoyed my book. I love to hear from readers!

Facebook:

http://www.facebook.com/authormaryannjordan

Facebook:

http://www.facebook.com/lostinromancebooks

Email:

lostinromancebooks@gmail.com

Email:

authormaryannjordan@gmail.com

Blog:

http://www.lostinromancebooks.com

This information on Rheumatoid Arthritis is from the Arthritis Foundation (www.arthritis.org).

"Rheumatoid arthtitis (RA) is an autoimmune disease in which your body's immune system …mistakenly attacks your joints. The abnormal immune response causes inflammation that can damage joints and organs, such as the heart. Early diagnosis and prompt treatment is the key to preventing joint destruction and organ damage."

"Nearly three times as many women have the disease as men. In women, RA most commonly begins between ages 30 and 60."

"There is no cure for RA, but there are a number of medication available to help ease symptoms, reduce inflammation, and slow the progression of the disease."

For those of us who suffer from RA, please be aware that we strive for a normal, healthy life, living with the challenges it may bring (for an author, that includes typing). If you are interested in more information, please visit the Arthritis Foundation website.

Maryann Jordan

21553014R00186

Made in the USA
Middletown, DE
03 July 2015